THE GHOSTS OF SALEM VILLAGE

THE GHOSTS OF
SALEM VILLAGE

Scott M. Baker

Also by Scott M. Baker

A Schattenseite Book

The Ghosts of Salem Village
By Scott M. Baker.
Copyright © 2021. All Rights Reserved.
Print Edition
ISBN-13: 978-1-7365915-0-5

Cover Art © Warren Design

A Note to My Readers

Please don't think I'm exploiting the horrors of the Salem Witchcraft Trials. I assure you I'm not. I have a strong attachment to Salem. I earned my History Degree from Salem State College (now Salem University) and worked two summers as a tour guide at the Essex Institute (now the Peabody Essex Institute). When coming up with a story for the second Tatyana novel, the trials provided the perfect background.

I have not whitewashed the fear that plagued Salem Village nor the proceedings themselves. Every chapter related to the events of 1692 was thoroughly researched and is as accurate as possible. My goal is to give my readers an accurate accounting of what happened and the injustices the nineteen victims endured. I did not dramatize history to enhance the plot but rather based my story on historical facts. Hopefully, I have provided my readers with a better understanding of that terrible period of history.

Eliza Adams is fictional. The character and everything that happens to her is a figment of my imagination. Her comments and thoughts on the trial were shared by some of the more rational residents of Salem Village.

Judge Corwin was a participant in the trials, but his actions were never recorded. As such, I have taken liberties with his parts in the novel. You will see why he is so vital to the story. This in no way is meant to detract from all the good he did for Massachusetts in his later years.

As for Sheriff Corwin, he is a historical figure. His participation in the fictional parts of this novel is based on his behavior as noted in the historical records. I believe I have portrayed the sheriff accurately. I'll let you be the judge.

CHAPTER ONE

"WE'RE GOING TO do it in a parking lot again?" Debbie crossed her arms and huffed as John, her boyfriend, pulled his ten-year-old Honda Civic into Forest River Park.

"It never bothered you before."

"What an ass." She shifted to look out the passenger window.

"Come on. I'm joking."

"Everything's a joke with you."

John placed a hand on her knee and squeezed. Debbie slapped it away and moved her legs closer to the door.

"I'm sorry. Really. I know I can be a dick sometimes."

"Sometimes? That's an understatement."

If the insult bothered John, he didn't show it, which pissed off Debbie even more. Her anger shot through the roof when John pulled into a parking space beside a black Ford Escape. Their friends Tom and Cindy sat inside. Cindy smiled and waved.

Debbie turned to John. "I told you I'm not into that type of shit."

"Relax. We're here for a party, not an orgy."

A knocking on the passenger window caught Debbie's attention. Cindy stood by the window, motioning for her to lower it. When she did, Cindy leaned inside and hugged her friend.

"It's so good to see you."

Tom came over carrying a case of Coors under his arm, high-fiving John as he climbed out of the sedan. "You ready?"

John tore open the top of the case, pulled out a can, popped the top, and raised it in a toast. "Let's get this party started."

Debbie stepped out into the parking lot and glanced around. Forest Hill Park sat on the shore of Salem Harbor. It was an open area exposed for hundreds of feet. Nearly a dozen houses lined two sides of the park. The playground in front of them and the hill behind with a scant covering of trees offered little protection. Anyone who lived in those houses could see what was going on. Any cop coming out of West Avenue had a clear view of everything. Being the only two vehicles in the parking lot would draw a lot of attention, something none of them wanted during a beer binge since the oldest of them, Cindy, had only turned nineteen last month.

"We're gonna get caught if we stay out here," she warned.

Cindy took her arm. "That's why we're not drinking out here."

"Then where are we drinking?"

"In there." Tom pointed in front of him as he headed down a cement walkway.

"There" referred to a copse of trees in front of them. A six-foot-high fence composed of wooden slats ran along the edge of the tree line. At the end of the walkway stood an entry gate. Above it hung a wooden sign that read:

PIONEER VILLAGE Salem in 1630

"What is this place?" asked Debbie. "I've never heard of it."

Cindy giggled. "No one has."

"It was built to celebrate Salem's three hundredth anniversary," answered Tom. "It supposedly looks the way Salem did during its first years. The city never tore it down. It eventually became a tourist attraction."

"How do you know all this?" asked Debbie.

"My older brother worked here last summer. He told me about it. Even better than that...." Tom reached into his pocket and withdrew something. "He gave me the key to get in."

Tom passed the case of beer to John then slid the key into the padlock. With a quick twist, it popped open. He looked at the girls and winked. Tom ushered them inside, closing the gate behind him.

A duck pond sat to their right. They walked for several yards, crossing a tiny footbridge and entering a clearing. A one-room wooden building sat on the opposite side.

"What's that?" asked Cindy.

"It's the gift shop," Tom answered. "If you take off your shirt, I'll think about getting you a new one."

"No, you pervert." She playfully nudged him in the chest with her elbow. "I mean, what's in front of the gift shop."

"They're pillories. Back in those days, if you were found guilty of a crime, you'd be placed in one of them in the town square so everyone could see your shame."

"I want to try." Cindy ran over to it.

Tom joined her. He lifted the upper board. Cindy placed her head in the larger groove and her wrists in the two smaller ones on either side. Tom lowered the board, trapping her.

"Someone take a picture."

John placed the case of beer on the ground and removed his cell phone. Lining up the shot, he snapped a photo. The flash blinded them temporarily.

Debbie punched him in the arm. "Are you crazy? Someone might see that and call the cops."

"Relax. You're too wound up."

Cindy tried to pull free but couldn't. "Get me out of here. It's uncomfortable."

"It's supposed to be." Tom walked over and paused. "What's in it for me if I get you out?"

"If you don't get me out of here, you're not getting any tonight."

"Fair enough." Tom moved around to the back. Instead of

lifting the upper board, he shoved his crotch against Cindy's ass and began dry humping her from behind.

"Stop that!"

Tom continued his foolishness. "Hey, get a video of this."

"No!"

John took out his cell phone again.

"That's it," said Debbie, heading for the walkway. "I'm waiting in the car."

John rushed after her and stopped her at the bridge. "Come on. We're just having fun."

Debbie turned her back on him and crossed her arms over her chest again. John tried to hug her from behind. She pushed him away.

"I'm sorry. I'll be good."

Debbie couldn't stay mad at him. She spun around and kissed him. "Okay. But watch it. We could get into big trouble for being here."

John took her hand and led her back to the others. Tom had already released Cindy. She couldn't have been too angry, considering he had her pressed against the pillory with his hand up her sweater. On seeing their friends, they broke the embrace and straightened their clothes. Tom picked up the beer.

"Follow me."

They crossed another footbridge, eventually stopping in front of a two-story wooden building. The sign listed it as the Governor's Mansion. A run-down fence made from tree branches tied together with rope surrounded the property. Directly across from it sat a garden, enclosed by a similar old-style fence. Two modern benches stood by the gate. Tom placed the case on one of the benches and removed three cans, handing one to each girl and keeping the last for himself. The girls sat down and drank. John finished off his Coors, pulled a second from the box, popped it open, and took a long gulp.

Debbie scanned the area. "Is this where they burned the

witches?"

"Sure is." John spun around. Beer spilled from the top of the can onto his hand. "Right on this very spot."

"Don't listen to him," said Tom. "The witches in Salem weren't burned. They were hung."

"Like me." John grabbed his crotch.

Tom ignored him. "They burned witches in Europe, not here. Those killed in Salem were hanged on a hill near Walgreens."

"But not here?"

Tom shook his head. "This place was a forest back then."

"Look at you," teased Cindy. She stood and wrapped her arm around his shoulder. "Good looking and smart. I hit the jackpot."

"Yes, you did." He leaned into Cindy and kissed her.

An uneasiness suddenly settled over Debbie. Something about this place did not feel right. Cold seeped under her skin, and not all of it was due to the weather.

"I don't feel comfortable here." She met John's gaze.

"Have another beer. That'll warm you up."

"I don't want a beer," she snapped. "I want to go home."

Cindy reached over and clasped her friend's hand. "Are you okay?"

"No. I have a bad feeling about being here."

Cindy turned to Tom. "Maybe we should go."

He nodded in agreement. "John, let's find another place to drink."

"You're all a bunch of pussies." John finished his beer, tossed the can aside, and removed a third.

"Come on. We can drive down to Nahant—"

"Warlock!" John stepped back and pointed at his friend, then broke into a drunken laugh. "You're possessed."

"John," said Debbie. "Stop it."

"Witch!"

Tom had enough. He tapped Cindy on the shoulder.

5

"We're out of here. Debbie, do you want a ride?"

"Thank you."

John dismissed them with a wave of his hand. "You're a bunch of Purigrims."

"Puritans," corrected Tom. He grabbed the case of beer and walked away. They fell in behind him.

"Wait. Wait." John picked up a stick in the shape of a Y. As he stepped toward the Governor's Mansion, he reached into his pocket, removed a lighter, and placed the flame against the wood. After a few seconds, the top of the stick caught fire. He held it in front of his chest. "What am I?"

Tom sighed. "I don't know."

"I'm a witch."

Debbie grimaced. "That's sick."

John laughed. He moved the stick in a circle and bounced it up and down, mimicking a scream as he did so as if it were a person on fire.

Tom took Cindy by the hand. "Let's go."

"Hold on." Debbie stepped closer to the Governor's Mansion.

"Leave him. He's an asshole."

"I don't care about him." Debbie pointed to the building. "What's that?"

All of them turned to the structure. A brilliant light shone inside. At first, they feared it might be a night watchman. Yet the light didn't appear as though it came from a bulb but rather a candle. Only Debbie had never seen a candle generate this much illumination.

The light passed by one of the windows on the second floor, moving into the hall and descending the stairs. It dimmed for a moment, then brightened again when it reached the first floor, growing more intense as it neared the exit. Rather than the door opening, the light passed through the wood, emerging as a fluorescent, hovering sphere that drifted above the ground.

Debbie took a few steps back. Every rational part of her

brain told her to run, but curiosity had gotten the better of her. She needed to know what was inside the sphere.

It floated across the yard toward John and began to morph, developing what appeared to be arms and legs. As it drew closer, the shape became more defined and gradually took on the form of a young woman in her mid-twenties. She wore a dark-colored dress made of wool that hugged her physique, but not in a sensual manner. A white apron tied around her waist draped down to her knees. A white collar hung around her neck, partially covered by her disheveled and pulled-back blonde hair. The image never took corporeal form, shimmering like a hologram. It stopped ten feet from John and examined him, shifting its head from one side to the other.

"G… guys." John could not divert his gaze from the image hovering in front of him. "Please tell me this is part of a light show."

"Back up slowly," advised Debbie.

John ignored her. He reached out a hand and extended it toward the spectral image. It pulled back a few feet and paused, staring at him. John moved closer. This time she allowed him to touch her. His hand passed through. John jerked it back.

"What's wrong?" Debbie asked.

"It's cold. Like sticking your hand into iced water." John held his hand over the burning stick to warm it.

The spectral image focused its gaze on the stick. Its eyes widened, then shifted onto John. The cool, white glow darkened, taking on a harsh, yellowish hue. Its eyes glared red and locked onto him. The pretty face of the young woman shifted into a horrifying visage. Its hair became scraggly, the skin charred and blistered, the mouth distorted with blackened teeth. Surging forward, it stopped inches from John's face and howled, a scream half fury and half agony.

"Move!" Tom practically dragged Cindy toward the exit.

John emptied his bladder and his bowels. Debbie ran forward, grabbed his arm, and yanked him away. She cast a glance over her shoulder, praying the thing wasn't following them. It stood where they had left it, the terrifying appearance still on its face, its blood-red eyes fixed on her.

The spirit collapsed into a glowing mist that blew away in the wind.

CHAPTER TWO

TATYANA OPENED THE door and stepped into the front hall of the two-story home. The interior was cold and dark. Removing the flashlight that she carried in her pocket, Tatyana switched it on and directed it across the wall until the beam landed on the light switch. She flipped the first switch on the left. Nothing happened. She tried the next two with the same results. The electricity had been disconnected, not that it surprised her given the circumstances of this case.

Tatyana was doing this for her friend Doreen. Well, not a friend but her realtor. Doreen had found her a sweet deal on a two-bedroom apartment in Hanover not far from Dartmouth College, and even negotiated the rent down two hundred dollars. When Doreen discovered that Tatyana performed paranormal investigations and cleansings on the side, she asked if Tatyana would help her friends, Richard and Linda. The two claimed something evil had moved into their house several years ago and had ruined their lives. In the past two years, Richard had lost his job at UPS due to a work-related injury and now relied on worker's comp. Since his accident, he had gained close to fifty pounds, developed diabetes, and, for the last year, had suffered from bedroom performance issues. Linda's depression worsened shortly after that, causing her to lose three jobs within a year, leaving her with a work record that prevented anyone from hiring her. Doreen confided that the couple, once happily married, had been fighting non-stop for over a year, mostly about finances, and considered separation. Tatyana had agreed to do a walk-through of their house

9

for free.

Taking a deep breath, Tatyana slowly exhaled, clearing her mind of all thoughts. She closed her eyes and opened her senses, trying to detect the aura of any spirit residing in the house. She picked up on a negativity that hung heavily in the air, but nothing supernatural. Tatyana homed in on it, hoping to detect a spectral aura. There was none.

"I'm addressing the entity or entities that reside in this house. Please answer me."

Still nothing.

Tatyana made her way into the living room and flashed the light around. The room was a mess. Clothes and shoes lay scattered across the floor and furniture. Piles of dirty plates and utensils sat on the coffee table along with more than a dozen empty beer bottles. Still no indications of a spirit.

Moving down the hall to her left, she stopped in front of the laundry room. Piles of unfolded clothes sat on the washer, dryer, and counter. No one had cleaned the toilet in the corner for months, with dark stains running down the front onto the floor and others covering the bowl's interior. She stepped over to the wall rack holding the brooms, mop, and cleaning supplies. Each had dust on them.

Continuing down the hall into the kitchen, she found the worse mess so far. Dishes and glasses filled the sink. Seven six-pack containers filled with empty beer bottles had been stacked by a garbage can overflowing with rubbish. Empty food containers, stacks of opened mail piled seven inches high, plus sundry other items filled every inch of counter space. Another set of dirty dishes filled one end of the kitchen table, the rest taken up by clothes and unopened Amazon boxes. The negativity in this room was intense.

"I'm addressing the entity or entities that reside in this house. If you are here, please talk to me."

A thump sounded on the counter to Tatyana's left, followed by a meow. She flashed the light toward it. A small black cat sat on the counter, reaching out and trying to get her attention with its paw. She petted the cat, which purred loudly and rubbed its head against her palm. She felt mats of clotted fur.

"Are you the evil spirit?" Tatyana joked.

After several minutes of affection, the cat jumped off the counter and disappeared through a cat door onto the back porch. Tatyana followed. A litter box sat between two piles of uncollected garbage. The box had not been cleaned in weeks. So much cat poop filled the box that the poor animal had taken to relieving itself on the tiled floor. No one had bothered to pick up the overflow.

A familiar voice called out from behind her. "What conclusions have you come to?"

Nick stood in the open door, his hands clasped behind his back, a wry smile on his face.

"I'm still investigating."

"I already know what the problem is here."

"Good for you." Tatyana did not attempt to hide her sarcasm.

"I want to see if we reach the same conclusion."

Tatyana placed one hand on her hip and flashed him a frustrated glare. "We can compare notes when I'm done. Now let me work."

Nick held up his hands in mock surrender. "Okay. I won't bother you."

Tatyana went back into the kitchen. She saw the door leading to the basement and headed downstairs. Turning the corner at the bottom of the steps, she entered a finished portion turned into an entertainment room. A large-screen TV dominated the opposite wall. The living area presented the same sloppy disarray as the rest of the house. Three pillows and two disheveled blankets on the sofa testified that someone, probably Richard, had been sleeping down here frequently. This part of the house felt darker and broodier than the first floor.

The unfinished portion contained the boiler, water heater, and an array of plastic storage bins and cardboard boxes. Half were in stacks. The other half lay scattered across the floor, opened, some of their contents strewn about. Strands of cat shit intermingled with the clutter.

"I'm addressing the entity or entities that reside in this house. Please, if you can hear me, make yourself known."

The only response came from the cat, which meowed as it rubbed against her leg.

Going back upstairs, Tatyana passed through the kitchen and climbed the stairs to the second floor. Two doors stood opposite each other on either side of the hall. She entered the door on the right, stepping into a guest bedroom. This room had been spared the messy indignity of the rest of the house. It had not been used in a while as testified by the thick layer of dirt covering the furniture.

She crossed over to the opposite room. This one had been converted into Linda's sitting room, at least judging by the feminine décor. A reading chair and antique floor lamp occupied the corner nearest the front window. The end table beside it contained a glass half-filled with iced tea and a paperback copy of Julia Quinn's novel *Bridgerton: The Duke and I*. Three bookshelves lined the interior wall, each sporting various knick-knacks and several dozen regency romance novels. Like the guest bedroom, this room was also tidy, especially when compared to the rest of the house.

Continuing down the hall, Tatyana opened the door and stepped into the master bedroom. The negativity in this room was extreme. She felt it pressing against her senses and, for a moment, depression overtook her. Tatyana quickly cleansed herself of that emotion, took a moment to center her thoughts, and shone the flashlight around the room.

The master bedroom made the rest of the house seem stately by comparison. Barely any of the floor could be seen through all the clutter and clothes thrown about. Unlike the rest of the house, the shades in this room were all pulled down, preventing outside light from entering. An unpleasant scent permeated the area, a combination of must and body odor. Dirty dishes and empty beer bottles covered Nick's nightstand. Linda's was cleaner but still in a state of disarray, with a collection of pill bottles filling one corner. Tatyana made her way across the room, careful not to step or trip over anything, and examined the bottles. Melatonin. Xanax. Zoloft. Abilify. Nothing for physical ailments, only depression and anxiety, which must also have started affecting Linda.

A meow came from the door. The cat stood at the opening, calling to Tatyana but refusing to enter the room.

Checking the master bath, she found it even more disgusting than the one in the laundry room. Neither the toilet, shower, nor sink had been cleaned in who knows how long. Clothes and used towels littered the floor. Cosmetics filled the counter until no space remained.

Only one word described this part of the house–disgusting.

"Meow," came a voice from the door.

"Really?"

"It's better than rubbing against your leg."

"You can try if you want to get neutered."

"It won't work. I'm a ghost." Nick entered the room. The cat followed, staring up at him in fascination. "Have you reached a verdict yet?"

"Yes." Tatyana sounded like a frustrated teenager agreeing with her mother. "There's no spectral entity here."

"I agree."

"Now to break the news to Richard and Linda."

Tatyana made her way downstairs, the cat chasing behind her. She bent down and petted the cat one final time before heading outside.

As she stepped off the porch, Doreen, Richard, and Linda climbed out of their cars and met her on the front lawn.

Doreen placed her hand on Tatyana's arm. "Are you

okay?"

"I'm fine."

"Did anything bad happen to you in there?" asked Linda.

"Nothing unusual took place."

Linda looked over at her husband and back to Tatyana. "You didn't sense the spirit?"

"There is no spirit in your house."

"You mean you weren't able to contact it?"

"There is no spectral entity in the house to contact."

Linda became even more confused. "What... what about the darkness and negativity we both experience in there? Didn't you sense that?"

"I did. There's a large negative presence residing in your house."

"What's causing it if it isn't a ghost?" asked Richard.

"You are." Tatyana noticed Richard bristle at the comment and immediately explained. "Negative energy can form in a location without the presence of a spectral entity. If there are a lot of bad emotions somewhere, such as anger, jealousy, or depression, over time those damaging feelings can form a destructive aura around a property, much like a house that is blessed is filled with happiness. Once that aura is created, it produces dark energy that causes those affected by it to become more miserable, and then feeds off that increased negativity."

"Is it dangerous?" asked Linda.

"Physically, no. However, it'll tear you apart spiritually and mentally unless you can reverse the trend."

Linda squeezed Richard's hand tightly. He rubbed her knuckles in comfort. "You mentioned something a minute ago about a blessed house being a happy house. Can we exorcise the bad aura by having the house blessed by a priest?"

"Unfortunately, no. You must understand that what you're experiencing is not an entity that has attached itself to you that I can drive away. What you're dealing with, for lack of a better phrase, is a really bad vibe formed from the negative feelings inside you. A blessing or cleansing won't help. Only you and your wife can reverse the situation. And it won't be easy."

"What do we have to do?" Richard placed an arm around his wife.

"We'll do anything," added Linda.

"The only way you can undo this is by changing your way of thinking and start viewing things more positively. From what you've told me, you're both going through some tough times. Don't focus your energy on that. Concentrate on what's important. The two of you. Getting back on your feet financially. Family and friends. Your cat."

Linda smiled. "You met Chocolate Munchkin?"

Tatyana nodded. "She followed me around the house begging to be petted."

"Really?" Richard glanced at Linda and back to Tatyana. "She's been avoiding us for months."

"That's part of the negative aura. Once you remove the feeling, she'll come back to you."

Linda sniffed back a tear.

"I know this isn't going to be easy for you, but you have to put a lot of effort into this. Otherwise, the negative aura will dominate your life. Do whatever you have to do to improve your situation. See a counselor, a therapist, a specialist, a financial advisor, anyone who might help get you through this."

"We will," promised Richard.

"Thank you so much." Linda hugged Tatyana, holding her for several seconds.

"One more thing," said Tatyana. "I would start with the house itself. Pick up the clutter, remove the garbage, clean it from top to bottom, and raise the shades. The aura feeds off a bad environment as much as it does emotions."

"I told you to pick up after yourself," whispered Linda.

Richard broke their embrace. "You're saying this is my fault?"

"No, I'm not. We're both respon—"

"Then why bring it up?"

Tatyana rolled her eyes and strolled back to her car, a midnight black Volkswagen Passat she leased. Doreen joined her.

"Thank you for doing this." Doreen leaned closer to whisper even though the others could not hear her. "I honestly had no idea how bad things had become here."

"Have you been inside?"

"No. I usually meet Linda somewhere in town for drinks."

"Trust me. You don't want to go in there."

The two women reached the Passat and stopped. As Tatyana opened the door, Doreen extended her hand. "Thanks again."

Tatyana shook it. "My pleasure."

"Do you think they'll be all right?"

Tatyana glanced over at the house. The disagreement had devolved into a full-blown argument, with Linda storming off into the house while Richard flipped her the middle finger behind her back. She shrugged.

"I hope so."

Climbing into the car and starting it, Tatyana pulled away from the house, happy to put that unpleasantness behind her. She barely drove a mile when Nick materialized in the passenger seat.

"You know as well as I do, those two aren't going to make it."

"I like to think the best of people. I'm an optimist."

"And I'm a realist."

Tatyana chuckled. "You're a pessimist."

"Do you blame me? My wife beat me to death with a fireplace poker."

"Okay, you win. They'll probably get divorced within a year. But at least I can hope."

Nick changed the subject. "We ought to stop at a Starbucks."

"Why? You're a ghost. You can't drink."

"I know. But you like Starbucks. I can't get physical pleasure out of life anymore, but it makes me happy to see you happy."

At first, Tatyana was going to protest, but then the idea of an iced espresso sounded appealing. "You got a deal. We'll stop and drink it somewhere where we can chat."

"I'd like that. I enjoy talking with you."

Tatyana chuckled.

"What's so funny?"

"Nothing." She kept her eyes on the road. "You're weird in a lovable way."

CHAPTER THREE

TATYANA AND NICK had parked at the scenic overlook near Exit 12 on I-89. The sky was clear of clouds and a full moon illuminated the slopes of the mountains to the northwest. Except for the few cars and trucks that drove past on their way north, the setting was peaceful and relaxing. Exactly what she needed. She nursed along her iced espresso, enjoying it now but knowing she would regret it in a few hours when she tried to sleep. Nick watched the couple in the BMW beside them making out and steaming up the windows, unable to take his eyes off them.

"You're a perv," she teased.

"No. It's been a long time since I've been with a woman."

"What do you call me?"

"That's not what I mean. I'm talking…." Nick struggled to find the right words, finally giving up and using his thumb to point over his shoulder to the couple who had begun undressing each other.

"You can live vicariously through me," said Tatyana.

"You have an active social life?"

"You're the first guy I've been with in years."

"Then I consider myself lucky."

Tatyana could not help but smile at the compliment.

Nick shifted in the seat, putting his back to the couple. "We've been ghost hunting for five months. Are you happy with it?"

"I am, though it's not what I expected."

"How so?"

"After confronting Kathleen, I expected the other cases to be more like *The Conjuring* or *Insidious*."

Nick raised his eyebrows. "And you're upset that you're not constantly battling the Netherworld from stealing your soul?"

"No. But you have to admit, the cases we've worked on are not the stuff of horror novels."

Nick nodded in agreement.

In the past five months, Tatyana had only taken nine cases, including the one she and Nick had gone on tonight. One had been a two-hundred-year-old house. It turned out that creaking and the opening of doors and cabinets was due to aging and settling, and that the cold spots resulted from a lack of proper insulation. Another house supposedly had been haunted by a ghost that traveled through the walls, only to discover that the spectral entity was a squirrel. Of the six cases that involved spirits, all were garden variety. The "worst" involved a pub in Manchester where the original owner had died of a massive stroke while cleaning up one night and still considered the place his property. Pappy stayed around, scaring the staff, occasionally knocking customers' drinks off the table, and once turning off the lights on the new owner, trapping him in the basement. With the new owner's permission, Nick worked out a deal with Pappy to stay around the pub as long as he didn't bother the staff. The owner set up a special booth reserved only for Pappy. Patrons swarmed to the place in the hopes of occasionally catching a glimpse of the ghostly former owner drinking a beer or wiping down the table. The others were spirits who needed guidance to the afterlife.

"Are you thinking of giving up cleansings?" asked Nick.

"Never. I enjoy helping the people who are haunted as well as the spirits. Besides, it's a nice break from studying all the time."

"And the money is good."

That Tatyana could not argue. She got paid two hundred and fifty dollars a case, which supplemented her income nicely.

Nick had returned his attention to the BMW beside them. The couple had gotten extremely intimate while she and Nick had talked. Tatyana leaned forward to see for herself. Meatloaf's *Paradise by the Dashboard Lights* played in her head.

"I can't believe they're doing that."

Tatyana chuckled. "You never went parking?"

"I did, but never in front of other people."

"The world has changed a lot since 1945."

"How?" Nick kept his attention on the BMW.

"Well, after World War II we fought a Cold War with the Soviet Union for another forty-five years."

"Figures. I never trusted the Russians. Did we win?"

"Yes and no. The Soviet Union fell apart on its own and became a democracy... sort of."

"Did we ever fight the Russians?"

Tatyana shook her head. "We were afraid to. Both sides possessed too many nuclear weapons to risk it."

"You mean like the ones we dropped on Hiroshima and Nagasaki?"

"Those were nothing compared to what we developed."

"Jesus." Nick shifted in his seat again to face Tatyana. "How did the world survive?"

"Good luck and world leaders who refused to use them."

"So, the world is at peace now."

Tatyana snorted. "You have a lot to catch up on."

"You'll have to let me use your computer."

"No problem, but not tonight. I have to get up early tomorrow and teach a class." Tatyana finished off her drink and started the Passat. "Time to head home."

As they pulled out of the parking space, the woman in the car beside them started screaming "Oh God" repeatedly.

"At least people have become more religious," said Nick.

Tatyana laughed. "You have *a lot* to catch up on."

✕   ✕   ✕

WHEN THEY REACHED Tatyana's apartment in Dartmouth, Nick said goodbye and disappeared. She missed him but knew he would be back tomorrow.

As she opened the door, Nostradamus, her Pitbull, came bounding out of the bedroom and ran around her, his tail wagging furiously.

"You were on the bed again, weren't you?"

Nostradamus stopped in front of his mistress and gave her the pouty eyes look.

"You know better than that."

The Pitbull stood on his hind legs, hugged her chest, and licked her face.

"I can't stay mad at you."

Nostradamus ran off and returned a few seconds later, clutching his favorite chew toy, a rubber ghost that squeaked. He chewed it by the refrigerator as Tatyana placed her stuff on the counter.

Tatyana had picked him up at the kennel. She had been looking for a dog that would protect her apartment from thrill-seekers and paranormal enthusiasts while she was away and warn her of any spiritual presences near her. Nostradamus was as dangerous as a newborn kitten, but having him around made her feel safe. It had taken the dog a few weeks to get used to Nick when he showed up. Now Nostradamus was as excited to see Nick as he was as to see her.

Opening the fridge, she gave him a boiled chicken strip from a Ziploc bag. Nostradamus took it and ran off to consume his treat. Tatyana slid off her jacket, draped it on the back of a kitchen chair, and stepped over to her answering machine. She had received three calls. One was from Kyle, her most ambitious student, saying he had the flu and wouldn't make it to class in the morning. One was pre-recorded message asking if she would be interested in an extended car warranty. She deleted that one immediately.

The third voicemail was much more interesting.

"Miss Reynolds, my name is Alison Bechtel. I'm the special assistant to Mayor Jenkins of Salem, Massachusetts. We'd like to hire your services. We have a ghost problem."

CHAPTER FOUR

23 March 1692
Salem Village

ELIZA ADAMS FILED into Ingersoll's Tavern along with most of the other residents of Salem Village. All those who entered the two-story structure were familiar with the place. It was the only drinking establishment around and, located on the main road between the village and Andover, offered lodging for weary travelers. However, those in attendance were not coming for the usual town meeting or to socialize. The reason for today's gathering was far more insidious.

The village leaders were about to put Rebecca Nurse on trial for witchcraft.

The nightmare had begun two months earlier when Elizabeth Parris, age eleven, and Abigail Williams, age nine, began to suffer afflictions. Samuel Parris was the village's Puritan minister. Elizabeth was his daughter. Abigail was an orphan who resided at the parsonage as a servant whom the minister treated as severely as his slave Tituba, whom he had brought with him from Puerto Rico. The young girls were confined to their beds but never recovered. When the village doctor visited, he had found nothing physically wrong with them, telling Parris they suffered from the effects of witchcraft. Parris did nothing but pray for their recovery and hope the issue would resolve itself. It did not. To determine what agitated the girls, Tituba had baked a Witch Cake, a biscuit made with rye flour and the urine of the afflicted person, which was then fed to a dog. If the dog exhibited the same symptoms as the ill person, the presence of witchcraft was "proven." Her efforts did nothing more than anger Parris to the point that he beat her mercilessly.

Over the next month, more young girls began to suffer from affliction: Mary Wolcott, Elizabeth Hubbard, Elizabeth and Alice Booth, Susanna Sheldon, Elizabeth Wilson, and Mary Warren, all teenagers. Anne Putnam, age twelve, who became the driving force behind the hysteria. And Sarah Bibber, a middle-aged mother and wife, and Anne Putnam's mother Ann, two adults who should have known better. In late February, the village magistrates ordered Parris to clean up his parish and cleanse Salem Village.

That was when the nightmare began.

The first women accused of witchcraft were outcasts that none of the villagers cared about. The slave Tituba. Sarah Good, a beggar with a bad temper. And Sarah Osborne, a widower once involved in a land dispute with the Putnam family. The General Court of Boston sent John Hathorne and Jonathon Corwin to oversee the proceedings. Both were devout men of the cloth with no judicial experience. Their only guidance on how to deal with witches came from *The Bible*, Exodus 22:18, which stated, "Thou shall not suffer a witch to live." Predictably, these three women were found guilty of consorting with witches and were imprisoned in Salem Jail.

Eliza and others in the village knew the girls were not afflicted but only seeking attention. One of the doubters was John Proctor, a local landowner who had vocally challenged the girls' integrity. A few days later, the girls accused his wife Elizabeth of witchcraft. That effectively silenced any opposition to what happened next.

Eliza never voiced her concerns about the false charges brought against these women. She knew none of them were witches but could not afford to reveal it.

Fueled by the town's lust for religious purity and the attention they received, the girls had accused two more women, both outstanding members of the community: Martha Corey and Rebecca Nurse. The court tried Martha two days ago, found her guilty of witchcraft, and sent her to Salem Jail.

Today was Rebecca Nurse's trial.

Villagers packed Ingersoll's. Rebecca had no business being here. She was seventy-one, frail, and sick, having been bedridden for over a week. An hour before her appearance, she had suffered the indignity of being taken to a private room in her nearby home where two midwives and Mrs. Ingersoll stripped the poor woman naked and examined her body for signs of the Devil. They had discovered an unusual protrusion on her vagina, the natural result of age and childbirth, and had listed it as evidence of a witch's teat. Now Marshall George Herrick assisted Rebecca into the tavern. Weak from illness and age, she used the bar to support her frail body. Frightened and confused, and hard of hearing, she would stand in front of her fellow villagers for consorting with witches.

The girls moaned upon seeing her, all but sealing the poor woman's fate.

Hathorne turned to the girls. "What do you say? Have you seen this woman hurt you?"

"Yes," cried out one of the accusers. "She beat me this morning."

"Abigail, have you been hurt by this woman?"

"Yes."

Anne Putnam cried out that Rebecca had also hurt her.

The judge turned to Rebecca. "Goody Nurse, here are two, Anne Putnam the child and Abigail Williams, who complain of your hurting them. What do you say to it?"

"I can say to my Eternal Father that I am innocent and God will clear my innocency."

Hathorne glared at her. "Here is never one in the assembly but that desires it. But if you be guilty, pray God discover you."

The trial continued. Various members of the community accused Rebecca of tempting them to sin or hurting them, or of afflicting children, all of which the poor woman denied.

Putnam yelled, "Did you not bring the black man with you? Did you not bid me to tempt God and die? How often have you ate and drank with your own demon?"

Hathorne focused on Rebecca. "What do you say to them?"

"Oh Lord, help me." Rebecca held up her hands.

The girls cried out and performed their act of suffering.

Hathorne asked, "Do you not see what a solemn condition they are in? When your hands are loose, the persons are afflicted."

Mary Wolcott and Elizabeth Hubbard accused Rebecca of hurting them as well.

"Here are these two grown persons now accuse you," said Hathorne. "What say you? Do not you see these afflicted persons and hear them accuse you?"

"The Lord knows I have not hurt them. I'm an innocent person."

"It is very awful to all to see these agonies. And you, an old woman thus charged with contracting with the Devil by the effects of it, and yet to see you stand with dry eyes when there are so many wet."

Rebecca answered the judge solemnly. "You do not know my heart."

"You would do well if you are guilty to confess and give glory to God."

"I am as clear as the child unborn."

Hathorne continued his questioning, asking Rebecca about her stomach illness, refusing to believe it was due to age, and pressing her on the charges against her, which Rebecca denied.

"They accuse you of hurting them," Hathorne said. "And if you think it is not unwillingly but by design, you must look upon them as murderers."

"I cannot tell what to think of it."

"Well then, give an answer now. Do you think these suffer

against their will or not?"

"I do not think these suffer against their will," Rebecca answered defiantly.

"Why did you never visit these afflicted persons?"

"Because I was afraid I'd have fits, too." Rebecca moved behind the bar.

All the girls cried in mock agony.

Hathorne looked at Rebecca. "Is it not an unaccountable case that when you are examined these persons are afflicted?"

"I have nobody to look to but God."

Rebecca tilted her head to one side. Elizabeth Hubbard twisted her neck in the same position.

Abigail yelled, "Set up Goody Nurse's head or the maid's head will break."

Someone from the crowd stepped forward and righted Rebecca's head. Hubbard's head immediately returned to normal.

Eliza realized it was the end for Rebecca.

A few more questions were asked, each time Rebecca proclaiming her innocence. Several people came to Rebecca's defense, but it was clear what the verdict would be. Hathorne pressured her to admit her guilt and be absolved, but Rebecca stood firm in her faith in God. In the end, Rebecca Nurse was found guilty of witchcraft and confined to Salem Jail.

The crowd left Ingersoll's Tavern, most convinced justice had been served, some believing these trials had gone too far but never publicly admitting as much for fear of being the next accused. Everyone felt confident the trials would continue.

Eliza slipped away unnoticed and rushed back to her two-room house on the northern edge of Salem Village, her conscience tearing her apart. She knew Rebecca and all the others who had gone before her were innocent of the charges. Worst of all, she could prove it and set them all free.

However, to do so would mean forfeiting her own life.

CHAPTER FIVE

T ATYANA CALLED ALISON early the following day and left a
voicemail letting her know she was interested in the case
and would call her back at two that afternoon. She held her
morning class and office hour right after, then returned to her
apartment to have lunch and prepare for the call. Part of the
preparation was summoning Nick. She wanted him to listen in
so she could get his thoughts on the matter.

At two o'clock, she called back Alison. The woman answered on the first ring.

"Is this Miss Reynolds?"

"Please, call me Tatyana. I assume this is Alison."

"It is." Relief was evident in her voice. "Thank you for
calling me back. The mayor is on my case to get this resolved
as quickly as possible."

"First, tell me what's going on."

"I can only fill you in on some of the details until you agree
to take the case and sign a Non-Disclosure Agreement. What I
can tell you is that two nights ago, four teenagers broke into
Pioneer Village to have a party and were attacked by...
something."

"What do you mean 'something'?"

"The police searched the area, thinking it might have been
a bear, but found nothing. They wrote it off as other teenagers
pranking the kids."

"But you don't believe that," said Tatyana.

"No. The kids claimed they encountered a ghost."

Nick caught Tatyana's attention. "Could they be lying?"

"Is it possible the kids are pulling a prank of their own?" she asked.

"Doubtful. I talked to the arresting officer who said the kids were scared half to death. If they're pulling a stunt, they're damn good actors."

"Was anyone hurt?"

"Not physically. But they're traumatized. One of the girls hasn't left her room since the incident. The police booked them on trespassing, possession of alcohol by minors, and two charges of public drunkenness, then released them to their parents' custody. I chatted with the parents yesterday. They all said their kids were terrified by what had happened."

Nick pretended to take a long swig from a beer bottle.

"Any chance they were drunk?" asked Tatyana.

"That was my first thought at first, especially when I heard the charge of public drunkenness. But one of the girls, the one who refuses to leave her bedroom, had nothing to drink that night. And drugs were not involved. That's not all." Alison hesitated. "We've had several reports of paranormal activity at Pioneer Village, though not to this extreme. Most of it is tourists insisting they saw a ghost or experiencing doors opening on their own or similar phenomena. Some of the people in nearby houses claim to have seen or heard things coming from the site that's unexplainable. A month ago, one of our tour guides quit because she felt her life was in danger, insisting something evil haunted the spot."

"How long has this been going on?"

"There have been isolated incidents since the city reopened the park in the late 1980s. Now we're getting on average one a week for the past seven months. This last incident made the local news. The mayor's afraid every amateur ghost hunter will be running around the property and wants to make sure nothing bad happens to someone else."

Tatyana chuckled. "Most people would consider me an amateur ghost hunter."

"Not according to your reputation."

The last comment caught Tatyana off guard. "What reputation?"

"I went on the Internet to find someone who could help. All the local paranormal investigation sites are talking about you. You're a celebrity in the community, which is why I chose you." Alison paused. "So, are you interested?"

Nick waved his hands to catch her attention as if constantly yelling, "Take it" was not enough.

Tatyana hesitated. Yes, this case sounded fascinating, and it would be more exciting than chasing down the spirits of grumpy old men. Yet, the memories of her confrontation with Kathleen at Eden Hollow remained fresh. She wasn't sure she wanted to go through that again.

"What are you doing?" pleaded Nick. "This sounds fun."

"I don't know," Tatyana said out loud.

Alison sweetened the pot. "The mayor's willing to offer you ten thousand dollars, half when you arrive and the rest when you've gotten rid of the ghost."

"It's a deal," said Tatyana.

Nick pumped his fist in the air.

"Thank you so much," answered Alison.

"When do you want me there?"

"If you could start tomorrow, that would be perfect."

Although short notice, for that type of money, Tatyana could easily re-arrange her schedule.

"I'll drive down later today."

"Perfect." Alison practically squealed with excitement. "I'll book a room for you at the Hawthorne Inn in the center of town. We'll meet in the lobby at nine tomorrow morning."

"Sounds good. See you then."

Tatyana pressed the End Call button and placed the phone on the kitchen table.

Nick slid into the chair opposite her. "Thank you."

"Why are you so excited about this job?"

"I've always wanted to see Salem."

"You're a spirit. Can't you go there on your own?"

"I could, but it's more fun when you're with someone." Nick grinned. "This is going to fun."

Tatyana wished she had Nick's enthusiasm.

CHAPTER SIX

THE RIDE TO Salem had taken over two hours. Nick and Nostradamus accompanied Tatyana, the latter curled up asleep on the back seat. Nick sat up front, staring out the window in awe. He had remained unusually silent until they crossed the border into Massachusetts.

"This is amazing," he muttered.

"What is?"

"These roads. They're huge. Do you know how long it would have taken me to drive this many miles back in my day?"

"A lot has changed since your day. Not all of it for the better."

"Like the style of your cars."

Tatyana snorted a laugh. "What do you mean? Cars today are awesome. Heated seats, power steering, satellite radio, built-in GPS."

"I'll grant you they're more comfortable, but the exteriors are boxy. They have none of the charms of an old '38 four-door Nash sedan or '40 La Salle Cadillac."

"You should have been around for the 1950s. Those were classy-looking cars."

"Really?"

"Nothing outclassed a '57 Chevy. Or a Porsche 356."

"A Porsche?" Nick stared at her dumbfounded. "They made tank engines for the Nazis during the war."

"Now they make some of the most expensive cars on the road."

"Wow." Nick went back to staring out the window.

Finding downtown Salem would have been difficult without the GPS. Once off the main highways, several secondary roads wound their way to Salem. Soon they were traveling through residential areas comprised mostly of late 18th and early 19th century houses that once belonged to the city's wealthy inhabitants who made a lucrative living off Salem's trade with Asia and the Caribbean. The guidance system took her down Derby Street. Several shops offered Tarot readings or minerals and stones used to ward off spirits. She was surprised to see signs for haunted tours of the city and directions to the Salem Wax Museum and Salem Witch Village. Salem had embraced its dark heritage.

Alissa turned left onto Hawthorne Boulevard. The Hawthorne Inn stood one block away. It was a six-story brick structure built in the 1920s and the most famous accommodations in the city. A red brick sidewalk circled the building. Lime green awnings hung over the windows on the first floor. She had checked out the location on Google Maps, pleased to find it centrally located to the areas she needed to visit. As icing on the cake, the hotel appeared much fancier in reality than it did on the website.

Tatyana pulled into the parking lot behind the hotel and shut off the engine. Nostradamus lifted his head. On seeing that they had stopped, he looked out the window and wagged his tail.

"Yes, we're here, boy."

"Are you going to take me for a walk?" quipped Nick.

"I'd ask you to watch the car, but you'd probably scare anyone who tried to break in."

"It would deter crime." Nick flashed her a malicious grin. "I want to get a feel for the area. I'll meet you in the room later."

Nick disappeared, leaving behind a small mist.

"I hate it when he does that."

Tatyana attached the leash to Nostradamus' chest harness and let him out, retrieved her luggage from the trunk, and circled around to the side entrance. The lobby was elegantly designed with a carpeted floor, mahogany furniture, and blue or beige sofas and chairs.

She walked up to the front desk. A young woman greeted her with a smile. "Are you here to check in?"

"Yes. I'm Tatyana Reynolds. Alison Bechtel booked a room for me."

"We've been expecting you. We have you in Room 626 on the top floor overlooking the Commons. It's our best room."

"Sounds nice." Tatyana reached for her wallet. "I assume you'll need my credit card."

"Nope. The city is taking care of everything."

"Even better."

The young woman handed her two keycards and then glanced over to the concierge desk. "Simon."

A tall, lanky young man rushed over.

"Could you please take Miss Reynolds to her room?"

"Of course." Simon picked up her suitcase, travel bag, and knapsack.

"My name's Sophia. I'll be on duty for the next three hours. Please call down if you need anything."

"Thank you."

"If you'll follow me." Simon headed for the elevator. Tatyana fell in behind him. Nostradamus followed, sniffing everything he passed.

"Are you here for business or pleasure?" Simon asked.

"A little of both. I've never been to Salem before. It looks like a lovely place."

"It is, but I'm partial. I was born and raised here." Simon pressed the button on the elevator. The doors slid open. He ushered Tatyana inside and pressed the button for the sixth floor.

"You must know a lot about the history of Salem."

"I do. The hotel was named after Nathanial Hawthorne. He worked at the Customs House while he wrote *The House of Seven Gables*. Most people don't know that Nathaniel was a relative of Judge Hathorne, who conducted the Salem Witch Trials. He added the W to his name because he didn't want to be associated with that part of the city's history."

The elevator stopped on her floor. Simon let Tatyana and Nostradamus exit first then stepped out. "Your room is this way."

"How much do you know about the trials?"

"Not too much. My focus is mainly on the city's maritime history. Did you know at one point Salem was a bigger and more active port than Boston?"

"I didn't."

Simon stopped in front of Room 626, opened the door, and stepped aside so Tatyana could enter. Two queen beds lay against one wall facing a pair of windows covered with silky white curtains. The room had an airy feel between the white linens and ceilings and the walls covered in decorative light-grey wallpaper. Nostradamus raced in and immediately claimed the bed closest to the bathroom as his own.

Simon stepped in and placed the luggage in the bedroom as he pointed out the various amenities available. When finished, Tatyana handed him a five-dollar bill.

"Thank you for everything."

"Thank you." He slipped the money into his pocket. "If you want, I can take your dog for a walk while you get settled in."

At the sound of the magic word, Nostradamus barked once and wagged his tail.

"Are you sure you don't mind?"

"It's my pleasure. He seems like a friendly guy."

"Too much so." She handed Simon the leash. "Just be careful. He tends to take me for a walk."

Simon crouched down and scratched Nostradamus' head.

"We'll be fine, won't we?"

The dog licked Simon's face and headed for the door.

When Simon and Nostradamus left, Tatyana strolled over to the closest window and lifted the pane. A cool breeze blew in, carrying with it the briny smell of seawater. Her room overlooked Salem Common. A massive Ouija board, large enough for people to stand inside the planchette, had been erected on the grass. Ironic considering her reason for being here.

Tatyana closed her eyes and opened her senses, seeing if she could detect any spectral signs coming from the area. A hum came from the city. She did not find that surprising considering all the ghost stories associated with Salem. But nothing intense, angry, or hateful, which astonished her. Considering all the people accused and executed for witchcraft, she expected a much deeper aura. Tatyana mentally called out to the spirits. The only response she received came from a ten-year-old girl buried in a nearby cemetery who had died of Tuberculosis in 1723. Maybe the dark specters avoided this part of the city. Maybe she had to be closer to where they died. Or maybe there were none. She would determine that tomorrow after she had Alison show her around.

A knock sounded on the door. Tatyana called out, "It's open."

Simon entered with Nostradamus. The dog ran to his bed, jumped on the mattress, and groomed himself.

"I hope he wasn't any trouble?"

"None at all. Though he claimed every tree in the Commons as his own."

Tatyana sighed and shook her head. She handed the young man a twenty-dollar bill.

Simon bowed graciously. "Thank you, ma'am."

"You're welcome. I have a question for you. Have you ever heard of any spectral activity down at Pioneer Village?"

"You mean ghosts?"

Tatyana nodded.

"There are hundreds of stories of ghosts haunting locations throughout Salem, including that spot. A few nights ago, four kids were arrested for trespassing there. They claimed to be attacked by a spirit. The cops think they were either drunk or made up the story."

"What do you think?"

Simon hesitated a moment. "If it's true, it's the first time any ghosts in Salem acted violently."

"You've been a big help."

"My pleasure, ma'am. If you need anything, call down to the concierge desk. I'm here until midnight." Simon left, closing and locking the door behind him.

Tatyana crouched beside Nostradamus and petted him. "Did you have fun?"

He licked her face then spread out across the closest queen bed.

Nostradamus had the right idea. Tatyana planned to eat dinner in the restaurant downstairs, then would take a shower and rest up for tomorrow.

CHAPTER SEVEN

2 June 1692
Salem Village

ELIZA ENTERED THE second floor of the Salem Town House where so many other villagers had already gathered. The atmosphere was solemn, though a sense of excitement buzzed through the crowd. Today would be a pivotal day in the ongoing witch hunt that plagued the village. Eliza harbored no illusions about what the outcome would be.

In the ten weeks since the trial of Rebecca Nurse, the situation had spiraled out of control. The day after her hearing, five-year-old Dorothy Good had been tried and jailed for being a witch. John Proctor, who had angered the Putnams over a land dispute, had been overheard at Ingersoll's Tavern complaining the accusers were merely seeking attention and needed a sound thrashing to bring them in line. A few days later, a warrant had been issued for his wife Elizabeth for engaging in witchcraft. Fear spread rapidly as an increasing number of people were accused, so many that Salem requested to imprison some in Boston Jail due to lack of room. Fear turned into dread when Abigail Williams claimed she had witnessed forty witches holding a Black Sabbath behind the parsonage and consorting with the Devil's representative, a black man in a hat. By the end of May, both jails were packed with men, women, and children tried by Judge Hathorne and found guilty of delving into the black arts.

On 27 May, the governor of Massachusetts had established a Court of Oyer and Terminer to hear the cases and determine their fate. Everyone in Salem Village now gathered to attend the first hearing.

Among those to stand trial was Bridget Bishop. The woman, now fifty-five, was the least Puritan of those accused, having been married three times and having numerous run-ins with the village magistrates. Bridget and her second husband, Thomas, had a volatile relationship, including arguments in public and physical violence against each other. It had gotten so bad the village had publicly whipped the couple to teach them a lesson. They did not learn it and were arrested later for the same crime. Thomas' daughter from a previous marriage bailed him out. Bridget had been forced to stand in the middle of the village commons wearing a sign on her forehead listing her transgressions. Earlier, she had owned an illegal tavern in Salem Town that the magistrates shut down after complaints from her puritanical neighbors. In addition, she had been accused several times of theft and once, in 1679, of witchcraft but was never tried. Nor did it help that Bridget Bishop was a bad-tempered woman who made numerous enemies over the years. At her trial, she had been accused of the death of livestock and children, of having her specter immorally attack men, and of hiding in the wall of her house poppets, crude dolls witches used to curse their victims. Not surprisingly, Hathorne found her guilty and sent her to jail.

Eliza had hoped that the court officials would be less inclined to believe the false charges and would try the cases with some modicum of justice. She was sorely mistaken. The judge and jury, comprised of residents of nearby towns, paid attention only to the depositions and physical examinations recorded by Hathorne and accepted as bona fide evidence the accusers' theatrics at the presentation of each witness. They even ignored the confession of one of the accusers, Mary Warren, who noted that the girls were so distracted and embedded in their fits they had no idea what they were saying.

Bridget Bishop's turn arrived. She had been stripped naked

and examined by midwives who had found a teat near her anus. A re-examination a few hours later discovered the teat had shriveled and dried, proof her familiar had sucked on it to get rid of the evidence. As everyone watched, Bridget was dragged from the jail into the court by two guards, her hands bound together, and forced to stand at the bar.

"Goody Bishop, you have tortured, afflicted, pinned and consumed, wasted, and tormented Mary Lewis, Betty Hubbard, Anne Putnam, Mary Wolcott, and Abigail Williams."

The girls began their charade, accusing Bridget of afflicting them, choking and biting them, and attempting to force them to sign the Devil's Book. The litany of charges continued. Bridget was accused of murdering people she did not like. Her specter had tried to drown a young girl in the river. She had threatened another with being beaten with iron rods. The charges included killing livestock and children, causing accidents, of hiding poppets in the walls of her house with pins inserted in them. Through it all, the wailing and theatrics continued, influencing the jury. Seven times Bridget confronted the girls on the accusations against her, claiming her innocence. Seven times the judge responded, condemning her for lying to the court.

Once the farce concluded, the judge advised the jury.

"The matter is in your hands now. Do not look for evidence of innocence. You are not mind whether the bodies of the said afflicted were really pinned and consumed, as was expressed in the indictment, but whether the said inflicted suffered such afflictions from the accused as naturally tended to their being pinned and consumed, pinned, and wasted. This a pinning and consuming in the sense of the law."

The verdict came as no surprise. The jury found Bridget Bishop guilty of witchcraft and sentenced her to hang.

Bridget was led back to jail, distraught and thoroughly defeated.

Eliza left the courtroom along with the other spectators.

Instead of returning home, she wandered down to the docks and found an isolated section of beach where she could think.

Eliza's mind tormented her. She could end this and spare that poor woman's life. All she had to do was go back to the court and reveal her secret to the judge. If she didn't, then she would be no better than those thrill-seeking girls who saw no problem with sending an innocent person to their death. Every part of her heart and mind told Eliza to do what was right despite the inevitable consequences.

Yet those consequences were what held her back. Eliza realized the fate that awaited her if she disclosed the truth. While she wanted to do the correct thing, fear prevented her. She had done nothing wrong, committed no crimes. She was far less guilty than Anne Putnam and her cabal. Yet revealing the truth would surely result in her demise. Was she a bad person for wanting to live?

Was she a bad person for allowing others to die so she may live?'

Eliza struggled with those thoughts until the sun began its slow descent. Not wanting to be caught outside alone at night, she headed back to her home, the inner conflict still playing itself out.

CHAPTER EIGHT

AFTER HAVING BREAKFAST and taking Nostradamus for a walk, Tatyana returned to her hotel room to get dressed. She chose a red dress and matching heels as well as a light leather jacket.

"You look lovely today." Nick stretched out on the bed beside Nostradamus.

"Thank you." Tatyana's good humor soured. "I hope you didn't watch me while I was dressing."

Nick expressed overdramatic shock at the accusation. "Would I do that?"

"Yes."

"I plead the Fifth."

Tatyana rolled her eyes. "I wish I could put you in a bottle and summon you only when I needed you, like a genie."

"You always need me." Nick swung his legs on the floor and stood. "Besides, a genie would only grant you three wishes. I'm always around to help you."

"Yes, you're always around." Tatyana checked herself one final time in the mirror.

"You look stunning."

She appreciated the compliment but changed subjects. "Did you find anything on your walk around town last night?"

"Only that there are a lot of spirits in this city, even more ghost stories, but nothing evil."

"I got the same impression." Tatyana faced Nick. "I'm going to ask Alison to show me some of the locations associated with the witch trials. I hope you're going to join us. I want to compare notes later."

"See, you *do* need me."

Tatyana shook her head. She scratched Nostradamus behind his ears. He rolled onto his back, begging for a belly rub, which she supplied.

"I'm heading down to meet Alison. Catch up with me."

"I will."

Only one person waited in the lobby, an attractive woman seated on the beige sofa against the far wall. Tatyana guessed her to be in her late twenties or early thirties. She wore a tan skirt, matching blazer and flats, with a black silk blouse, and brunette hair down to her shoulders. A pair of pink-rimmed reading glasses perched on her nose as she read through pages from a manila file folder. When she lifted her head and spotted Tatyana, a smile spread across her face.

"Are you Tatyana?"

"I am." The woman stood and shook Tatyana's hand. "I'm Alison. It's a pleasure to finally meet you. You have no idea how grateful the mayor and I are that you agreed to help us."

"It's my pleasure." Tatyana sat on the sofa opposite Alison and pointed to the folder. "What are those?"

"The police reports from the night of the incident, including statements from the four teenagers involved. I thought it might be useful in your investigation. I also have an NDA for you to sign."

"I've never had to sign one of those before."

"I'm sorry to have to make you do it, but the mayor is insistent." Alison spoke sincerely. She leaned forward and whispered. "Not that it's going to do any good. The rumor mill has already gotten wind of this. Within a week, it'll be the top story on all the local media. That's why I want to get ahead of it."

Tatyana scanned the Non-Disclosure Agreement, signed it, and passed it back to Alison. Alison signed and dated the agreement, handed Tatyana the police reports, then went on her cell phone.

The reports went into detail about what each teenager experienced that night at Pioneer Village. Their stories were nearly identical, especially with regards to the entity they claimed to have witnessed. According to the arresting officers, the kids were either drunk or pulling a stunt. Alissa disregarded the inebriation aspect because one of the girls tested negative for alcohol. However, she had not ruled out that they had made up this entire incident to garner attention. She would get to the bottom of that later. However, if the teenagers were telling the truth, Tatyana would be dealing with a spectral entity as malevolent as Kathleen, and that scared her.

Alison hung up the phone. "I just wired five thousand dollars to your bank account. Please feel free to check if you want to."

"I trust you." Tatyana handed back the manila folder.

"Are you ready to see Pioneer Village?"

"Before we do that, I'd like to see some of the locations in town related to the trials so I can get a sense of the spiritual presence associated with them."

"We can do that. Most of them are within walking distance." Alison slipped the folders into a leather bag. She stood and swung it over her shoulder. "Follow me."

The two women exited the lobby, crossed Hawthorne Drive, and turned right toward the Salem Witch Museum.

"You're taking me to a museum?" Tatyana sounded disappointed.

"You can see that on your time. It's informative and offers a general history of the trials. What you want is a behind-the-scenes tour."

"Sounds like you don't put much stock in Salem's museums."

"Not at all." Alison became defensive. "Don't take that the wrong way. We're extremely proud of our history, which includes so much more than the trials. Our museums are among the best in the state. I'm not here to promote Salem's tourist industry. I'm here to assist you in cleaning up something that could hurt people as well as our reputation. You're not going to get the information you need standing in front of a historical display."

Tatyana liked Alison. She played straight.

The two women turned in front of the Salem Witch Museum and walked down Brown Street.

"What really happened during the trials? I've read several theories, including one that speculated mass insanity due to lead poisoning from the food the locals canned."

Alison frowned. "The city wishes it could blame what happened on some natural cause. The truth is, nineteen people died because a group of children led by Anne Putnam decided it would be fun to be the center of attention for a while."

"Why?"

"No one knows what started it. Life for Puritan women in the colonies was harsh in the 17th century. They were entirely dependent on their husbands to support them. Children were ignored and did the household chores while their parents tended the fields from dawn to dusk six days a week. On Sunday, everyone was required to go to church for six hours, return home, and read the Bible. Abigail Williams, the ward of Reverend Parris, showed symptoms first. He put her to bed to rest. Then Parris' daughter joined in to get out of doing all the chores by herself. They went from being nobodies to being the center of attention in the village. Other girls heard about it and joined in. Soon it got out of control. The trouble began when Anne Putnam accused women she heard her parents gossip about, mostly those not popular in the village or those with whom the family had land disputes. Here's our first stop."

They stepped into the rear parking lot of the Peabody Essex Institute. In front of them stood a two-story wooden structure from the late 17th century. It had two steep gables attached to the front roof, a large central chimney, diamond-paned windows with leaded casements, and a second-story overhang.

"This is the John Ward House," said Alison. "It sat across the street from Salem Jail during the trials. The residents watched the accused being dragged in and out every day for their trials and witnessed the condemned being carted away to be hanged. The house was moved to the institute in 1910 when the city renovated the area where it stood."

Tatyana walked up to the house and placed her hands on the front door. She closed her eyes and cleared her mind, opening it to any spirits associated with the house. Nothing could be detected.

"I'm talking to any spectral entities attached to this house. If you are there, please reach out to me."

None did.

"This house is clean."

"I'm not surprised. The institute gives tours of the house and no one has ever reported a ghost."

Tatyana stepped over to Alison. "Is the jail still standing?"

"No. The city tore that down years ago."

"Can we go there?"

"It's our next stop."

They continued down Brown Street to the Witch City Mall and cut across the parking lot to the corner of Federal and St. Peter Streets. A large, two-story office building occupied most of the block.

"That's where Salem Jail was located." Alison pointed to the portion of the brick building against the intersection. She swung her finger to the church across the street. "The John Ward House stood there."

"When was the jail torn down?"

"A new jail was constructed in 1813. That was later converted into a house that the city tore down in the 1950s."

Tatyana crossed the street at the corner of the building. Again, she closed her eyes and opened her senses, this time detecting three spectral auras. Despair consumed the strongest.

Fear and unhappiness overwhelmed the second. The third merely existed with no emotional attachments and hovered around the first.

Alison came up behind her. "Do you sense anything?"

Tatyana explained what she felt. "Was anyone executed here?"

"No, but three prisoners died in jail before their trial. Sarah Osborne and Dorothy Good, who was five, died waiting for trial. Sarah Good gave birth to a baby girl, Mercy, who died within a few weeks."

Tatyana stared at her, incredulous.

"No one denies these were dark times," said Alison. She pointed across the street to the parking lot of Saint John the Baptist Church. "Over there was where they crushed Giles Corey."

"I thought all the accused were hanged?"

"Those that were found guilty. Giles was never tried. At that time, the law stated if you pleaded innocent and were found guilty, you forfeited your property. Giles was eighty-one years old and owned a hundred and fifty acres of land he willed to his sons-in-law. He refused to enter a plea, claiming the courts were siding against anyone who the girls accused. Sheriff Corwin attempted to get Giles to cooperate by making him endure *peine forte et dure*, a process where weights are placed on a person's body until they confess. They stripped Giles naked, laid him down in this empty lot, placed a board over his body, and slowly piled stones on it, one by one, but Giles refused to stand trial. The weight became so unbearable it pushed Giles' tongue out of his mouth, which Sheriff Corwin poked back in with his walking stick, laughing the whole time. On the second day, the weight became too much and crushed Giles."

"And he never entered a plea?"

"The only statement recorded was Giles taunting, 'More weight.' They hanged his wife Mary a few days later at Gallows Hill."

Tatyana crossed the street into the parking lot, expecting to be overwhelmed by Giles' tortured soul. Surprisingly, she sensed nothing. Nick wandered through the area. He glanced over and shook his head, confirming there were no spirits.

Alison joined her. "Are you picking up anything?"

"It's quiet. Considering how much anguish is associated with this spot, I felt certain I'd pick up something. No one has ever reported spectral sightings in this location?"

"Nothing that can be confirmed. According to urban legend, Giles' spirit walks the earth before a local disaster. There were reports of him roaming the streets before the Great Salem Fire of 1914. In 1978, he reportedly materialized again before then-sheriff Robert Cahill suffered a rare blood disorder, heart attack, and stroke within a year. Two previous sheriffs allegedly died from blood disorders or heart-related ailments while in office. Corwin himself died of a heart attack in 1696 while serving as sheriff. A legend has circulated for years that since Sheriff Corwin tortured and tormented Giles, Giles' spirit has sought revenge on every sheriff in Salem since. Nobody believed it. However, in 1991, Essex County moved the sheriff's office from Salem to Middleton. Since then, no sheriffs have died in office."

Alison motioned for Tatyana to follow and continued west along Federal Street.

"Do you believe these stories?" asked Tatyana.

Alison laughed. "Of course not. They're coincidences. But once an urban legend about the trials develops, it becomes fact. It comes with the territory of what happened here in 1692. My favorite 'curse story' involves Sarah Good and Reverend Nicholas Noyes. Noyes was the chaplain for the trials and, at one point, interrupted Sarah's testimony to condemn her as a witch. Sarah responded she was no more a witch than he was a warlock and warned that if they executed her, 'God will give you blood to drink.' Noyes died twenty-six years later of a brain hemorrhage that caused him to choke on his own blood."

They turned left onto Washington Street. Alison led Tatyana past the intersection with Lynde Street and stopped in front of 70 Washington Street. A four-story brick building sat on the spot with a career placement center occupying the corner office. Alison stopped in front of it.

"This is where the official trials were held. Those found guilty here were sentenced to death by hanging."

Tatyana stepped over to the wall and placed her hand on the bricks, opening her senses and mentally calling to any spirit willing to talk with her. No one from the spectral realm reached out. Clearing her mind, Tatyana felt for any negative energy flowing from this location. None existed.

"This area is clean."

"That doesn't surprise me," said Alison. "We've rarely had reports of hauntings associated with this area. I have one more place to show you before we go to Gallows Hill."

They continued along Washington Street for another block and turned right onto Essex Street. On the opposite corner stood the statue of Elizabeth Montgomery, who played the good witch Samantha on the TV show *Bewitched*.

"What would cause rational people to behave so barbarically?" Tatyana asked.

"No one knows for certain. As far as I can tell from my research, the Puritans came to America hoping for a prosperous life and one of religious purity free from harassment by the Church of England. Neither was the case. Within a few years, other communities surrounded Salem Village, which limited their ability to expand and grow more crops. Salem Town became prosperous due to its maritime trade while the village remained poor. The winters leading up to 1692 were harsh. And native American tribes in Maine, which at the time was part of Massachusetts, killed numerous people and disrupted life along the coast. The Puritans believed God was punishing them for sins they had committed and looked inwards for salvation. When the girls began blaming people of witchcraft, it gave the people of Salem Village the answer they wanted. Their troubles were not because of their own shortcomings but were the results of Satan coming after them. The accused became the scapegoats for the village's failures."

"You know a lot about this."

"I need to know what I'm talking about," Alison responded reluctantly. "It's tough enough dealing with this part of our history. I get two or three phone calls a month from people wanting to know details about the trials, from religious zealots wanting to be certain the brave people of Salem defeated the witches to some who want to do documentaries on how the trials are proof of America's hatred of women. I even had one Hollywood producer wanting to film an action movie here with an all-star cast about action heroes battling a coven of witches. I politely told them thanks but no thanks."

They stopped upon reaching the intersection with Route 114 and waited for the traffic signal. Across the road stood a three-story, 17th-century house with twin gables on either side of the entry hall and a central chimney. The design was similar to that of the John Ward House, only twice as large. Nearly thirty people stood in a line by the front door. The sign out front identified the building as the Witch House.

Alison pointed to it. "You'll find this interesting. It's the only building still standing in Salem directly associated with the trials. Judge Corwin lived here."

"The one who presided over the second set of trials?"

"The same."

The lights stopped the flow of traffic, allowing Tatyana and Alison to cross over. The moment Tatyana stepped onto the grounds, she detected a spectral presence, one filled with shame and self-loathing. It overwhelmed Tatyana, making her wince.

"Are you okay?" asked Alison.

"There's something here. Can we go in?"

"Of course." Alison led the way to the front door of the structure as those inside exited.

A young man in tan slacks and a sports jacket intercepted them. "I'm sorry, ladies, but you have to wait in line."

Alison produced her credentials for the attendant. "This is official business. We won't be long."

Grumbling came from those at the head of the line. Flustered, the young man did not know what to do. Alison took control. She turned to the tourists and pointed to Tatyana.

"I'm sorry, folks. This young lady is a producer from Hollywood who's considering doing a movie about the Salem Witch Trials. She wants to see the inside of the house. We'll only be a few minutes."

The group became amenable and voiced their approval. Alison thanked them with a charming smile and ushered Tatyana inside.

The interior portrayed how a wealthy Salemite would have lived in those times. They entered the main room, a dining area with a large fireplace dominating the wall to their left. Inside were several steel pots and cooking devices to show tourists how their ancestors would prepare dinner. Across from it sat a dining room table large enough to seat six, with brass and pewter plates and utensils laid out. Behind it stood two cupboards, the one against the window displaying a large copper platter.

Nick paused at the opposite end of the table, concern on his face. His eyes met Tatyana's. "Something bad is in here."

Tatyana stepped into the middle of the room. "The presence here is strong. Did all the personal items in this house belong to Corwin?"

Alison shook her head. "It's authentic to the time, but none of it belonged to the judge. The house went through numerous renovations over the centuries, but it was restored to its original design when the city moved it here in the 1940s."

"Where was the house originally?"

Alison pointed to the rear of the structure. "Only thirty-five feet away. The city moved it so they could expand the road."

"And most of the original structure is still intact?"

"Yes."

"That'll work perfectly."

Tatyana cleared her mind and senses. She detected the presence. Anger filled its soul. Not anger at her or anyone else. Bitter anger centered on itself. She mentally reached out to the entity, but it refused to engage her.

Alison started to speak, but Tatyana waved at her to remain silent.

"I'm speaking to the spirit who occupies this house. I know you're here. Please answer me."

Nothing.

"I'm not here to cleanse you or hurt you. I'm only seeking information. Will you talk to me?"

A pitiful voice came out of nowhere. "I will not."

Alison gasped and took a step back, stopping herself. Her face blanched. She quickly regained her composure.

"You do not have to reveal yourself."

The spirit did not respond.

"I'm a spirit like you," said Nick. He did not materialize so Alison could see him. "I know this woman well. She is not a threat to you. She's here to help. Please talk to her."

"If you insist. But I will not show myself to thee."

"That's fine," said Tatyana. "Are you one of the spirits condemned at the trials?"

"No."

"Do you intend us harm?"

"No."

"Then what are you doing here?"

"I live here."

"Are you Judge Corwin?" Tatyana asked excitedly.

A long pause ensued before the entity responded, its voice filled with shame. "I am."

"Why are you still here?"

"Because I know my fate if I leave this earthly realm. I will be condemned to eternal damnation for the sins I committed."

"What sins do you refer to?"

"We were wrong. So terribly wrong."

Tatyana chose her next words carefully. "What were you wrong about?"

"I tried my best," the spirit sobbed. "I always believed myself to be a man of God and tried to do his bidding. I failed miserably. So many innocent lives destroyed. And what we did to Eliza was unconscionable."

"Who is Eliza?" she asked.

"I refuse to talk about it. I will never live that down. I deserve no forgiveness."

"You must first be willing to forgive yourself," said Nick.

"I cannot. Thee has no idea of the sins I committed. I cannot forgive myself, nor can I expect the Lord and Our Father to do the same. I will talk with thee no more. Leave me to serve out my penance."

The entity retreated into the building. Tatyana sensed the hatred the spirit felt toward itself. Judge Corwin would no longer speak with them.

Alison stood motionless, her face blanched. "Wh-what just happened?"

"We talked to the spirit of Judge Corwin."

"You experience this all the time?"

"More often than you can imagine."

"And I thought my job was tough." Alison breathed deep and exhaled. Her color and composure slowly returned. "I think it's time I show you Gallows Hill."

CHAPTER NINE

WALKING BACK TO the Hawthorne Inn, they retrieved Alison's car and took Bridge Street across town to the local Walgreens. The summit of a hill rose behind the pharmacy. The barren limbs of the trees on its peak grasped ominously into the sky like the hands of the condemned reaching out to God.

"There it is," said Alison as they drove past Walgreens. "Gallows Hill."

She headed down Prospect Street, keeping the hill on her left, then turned left onto Pope Street. They passed a few residences before coming to a memorial erected at the base of Gallows Hill. Alison pulled her car off to the side of the road and parked.

Tatyana climbed out and studied the hill. With Salem being such a prime real estate market, she was surprised that no one had built a home on top of the hill. But then, who in their right mind would live on the spot where eighteen innocent people were hanged for witchcraft?

Nick wandered between the trees on top of the hill.

Tatyana opened herself to the tormented spirits she felt certain haunted the area. To her amazement, she sensed nothing. She followed Alison across the street.

A memorial sat at the base of Gallows Hill. A stone wall four feet high formed a semi-circle along the sidewalk. An inscription on the wall read Proctor's Ledge. Evenly spaced along the wall were eighteen marble plaques, each bearing one of the executed names.

Alison stopped in front of the memorial. "This is the actual site of the executions and not at the top of the hill as previously thought. This road used to link Salem Village with Andover. A local historian figured it out after reading eyewitness reports of those who saw the hanging bodies as they passed by, which they would not have been able to see on top of the hill. This memorial was built to honor the memory of the deceased."

A family milled around, the children reading the names on the plaques while the mother read about the site in a guide-book.

"May I do my thing?" asked Tatyana.

"Go ahead."

Tatyana cleared her mind and opened her soul but detected no spectral presence associated with the area, which shocked her considering this location's dark history. Starting with the plaque on the left, she touched the name of each victim and mentally called out to that person, requesting to speak to them. She sensed no spirits of those executed here. The family watched her intently.

Nick came down from the top of Gallows Hill and stood beside her. "There's nothing here."

"I know. I can't believe it."

"Can't believe what?" asked Alison.

"There are no spirits here from any of those executed."

"Excuse me." The mother came over to Tatyana. "Are you a psychic?"

"I'm a spiritual cleanser."

"Really?" The mother's eyebrows raised. "And you said there are no ghosts here?"

"Yes."

"That's not surprising," explained Alison. "History has proven that those accused, both those never tried and the eighteen executed, were innocent. Anne Putnam, the young woman most active in the accusations, later admitted their afflictions were a hoax to garner attention. Many of those involved, such as Judge Sewall, publicly confessed they erred in their handling of the trials. In 1702, the court declared the trials unlawful. Nine years later, the colony passed a bill restoring the rights and good names of those accused. The Puritan church reversed Rebecca Nurses' excommunication in 1712. In 1957, Massachusetts formally apologized for what had happened here in Salem. The accused were cleared of all charges against them in 2002. The city has done everything it could over the past seventy-five years to set the record straight and make sure their spirits are at rest."

"That's fascinating," said the mother.

"Have you seen the other sites in Salem?"

"No. We wanted to check this out first."

Alison reached into her pocket and removed four tickets. "These are all-access passes that will get you into the museums of Salem for free. Compliments of the mayor."

"Thank you. That's so kind." The mother took the passes, excited by the unexpected gift. She turned to Tatyana. "Good luck with whatever it is you're doing."

After the family piled into their mini-van and drove off, Tatyana asked, "What happened to the bodies of those executed?"

"They were tossed into a nearby gully and left to rot. Rebecca Nurse's family snuck in on the night of her execution, retrieved her corpse, and brought it back to her farm for a proper burial. She's buried on her estate in Danvers."

"And the others?"

"No one knows what happened to them."

"Is there any chance the bodies could have been disposed of at Pioneer Village?"

"It's possible." Alison thought for a moment. "But unlikely. The area is three miles from here, so it would have been difficult to transport so many corpses that distance. Besides, at the time there were many places nearby where they could have been buried." Alison paused. "Do you want to see Pioneer

Village now?"

"We'll do that tonight."

An expression of discomfort washed over Alison's face. "Why not now?"

"Spirits are more active at night. We have a better chance of encountering it and discovering what it wants if we go there around three in the morning."

"Why three?"

"It's considered an insult and taunt to Christianity. It's the opposite of three PM, the holiest hour of the day when Christ supposedly died on the cross."

Alison seemed skeptical. "Do you believe that?"

"The spirits do, so that's goo enough for me."

"I can arrange that." Alison's tone betrayed her nervousness.

"First, I want to talk with someone."

"Who?"

"The young lady who encountered the spirit the other night."

CHAPTER TEN

ALISON PARKED IN front of one of the elegant early 18th century homes along Chestnut Street that once belonged to one of the many merchants who made their living off Salem's maritime trade.

"I called ahead and talked to Mrs. Delillo," said Alison. "She agreed to let us come by but said it's up to her daughter whether or not she wants to talk to us."

"Let's hope for the best."

The women got out of the car and climbed the front steps of the house. Alison rang the doorbell. A few seconds later, an attractive middle-aged woman opened the door. She wore designer jeans and a grey sweatshirt with the Salem Witch Museum logo on the front.

"Are you Mrs. Delillo?" asked Alison.

"You must be the woman from the mayor's office."

"I am."

"Can I see your ID?"

Alison removed her city hall pass and handed it to the woman.

She studied it for a moment, handed it back, and opened the door. "Come in."

Tatyana stepped into a spacious foyer followed by Alison.

Mrs. Delillo closed the door behind them. "Sorry, but I have to be careful. I've had half a dozen reporters showing up at my door wanting to talk to Debbie about the other night. I refuse to let them in. I don't want my daughter to become the center of attention over what happened."

"I understand completely," Alison chuckled. "The press can be annoying."

Mrs. Delillo led the way up a grand staircase. "I told Debbie you were coming, but she says she doesn't want to talk with anyone. You can give it a try, but don't get your hopes up."

On reaching the second floor, she led them down the hall toward the back of the house. Tatyana immediately knew where they were heading by the piece of paper taped to one of the doors with LEAVE ME ALONE written in red magic marker. Mrs. Delillo knocked.

"Honey, it's me. Those women are here to see you."

"Tell them to go away. I don't want to talk to anyone."

"They're not reporters. Miss Bechtel is from the mayor's office."

"All they want to do is make fun of me like everyone else."

Tatyana stepped up to the door. "I'm a spiritual cleanser called in by the mayor to rid Pioneer Village of whatever is haunting it. I want to ask you a few questions about what you experienced so I know what I'm dealing with."

The sound of shuffling feet came from inside the room and the door opened a few inches. A pair of emerald-green eyes peered through the crack.

"You believe me?"

"I do."

"No bullshit."

Mrs. Delillo became embarrassed. "Language."

Debbie ignored her mother. "You're really from the mayor's office?"

"We are." Alison handed Debbie her ID.

The teenager examined it for a few seconds, passed it back, and opened the door. "I'll talk to you."

Mrs. Delillo excused herself. "I'll be downstairs if you need me."

Tatyana entered. Debbie's room was how she imagined any teenage girl's room would be. A desk with an open laptop and a shelf with books and various knick-knacks sat against the wall to the left. Between the two pieces of furniture sat a stand with a TV on top. Tatyana noticed a paranormal investigation episode paused on the TV. Three posters of music stars she had never heard of had been taped to the wall, making Tatyana feel old. A bed stood across from the desk, the headboard against the opposite wall. A dozen stuffed animals lay bunched around the pillow.

Debbie wore a pair of old sweatpants and a T-shirt emblazoned with Hello Kitty. A pair of cross-shaped earrings dangled from her lobes and a gold crucifix around her neck hung outside the T-shirt. She was an attractive girl for her age, with clear skin untouched by teenage acne and brunette hair cut in a bob. The only physical indication of what she had been through was her eyes, mostly expressing weariness from her ordeal but with a tint of fear in them.

Nothing about the teenager or her room suggested she dabbled in goth culture or satanism, which only confirmed for Tatyana that Debbie had witnessed a spectral event.

Debbie sat on her bed, picked up a stuffed unicorn, and held it against her chest.

"What do you want to know?"

Tatyana pulled out the chair from the desk and sat facing the teenager. "I read the police reports—"

"The police are useless. They wrote the whole thing off as a prank."

"The police aren't trained to handle these types of situations. I am."

"As I said in the report, we broke into Pioneer Village to drink. It was John's idea. I didn't want to."

"We're not judging you," comforted Alison.

"We were down near the Governor's Mansion when the spirit came after us. It started inside the mansion. We saw a bright light coming down the stairs from the second floor. At first, we thought it was a security guard coming to bust us.

Then it came through the door. I don't mean it opened the door. It floated through the wood and approached us. When it got close, it shifted from something that looked like a ghost to a demon with blood-red eyes and charred skin."

"Did anyone provoke it?" asked Tatyana. "Did anyone taunt it, throw something at it, do anything that might make it mad?"

Debbie shook her head. "Once it became angry, our only concern was getting out of there before it killed us."

"So, no one provoked it?"

"Not after it appear...." Debbie's eyes widened as she remembered something. "None of us told this to the police because we didn't think it relevant. Just before it showed up, John was being an asshole. He set fire to a twig that looked like a stick figure and made it run around like someone on fire."

Tatyana met Alison's gaze. "Were any of the accused burned at the stake?"

"No," replied Alison. "They were either changed, died in jail, or crushed to death like Giles Corey."

"You're certain about that?"

Alison nodded. "Nothing in the historical records indicates any of them were burned."

Tatyana focused her attention back on Debbie. "Can you describe what the spirit wore?"

"I can do better than that." Debbie placed down the unicorn, pushed herself off the bed, and stepped over to her laptop. Alison moved out of the way. The teenager called up the Internet and typed information into Google. "When everything settled down, I did some research on the clothes it wore. I found this."

Debbie shifted the screen so Tatyana could see. Alison peered over her shoulder. A drawing of a young woman dressed in late 17th century Puritan clothes filled the screen. The figure wore a dark-colored dress made of wool that hugged her form, a white apron tied around her waist, and a white collar and bonnet covering her neck and head.

Alison whistled. "That's the same style of clothes women wore in Salem in the 1690s."

"This case is getting more interesting by the minute," said Tatyana.

"Was that helpful?" asked Debbie.

"Yes and no. That picture raised a lot more questions than it answered."

Debbie appeared crestfallen. "Sorry."

"Don't be. You've been a big help." Tatyana tapped Debbie on the shoulder. "We're going to Pioneer Village tonight. How would you feel about joining us?"

Debbie's eyes widened. "Are you insane?"

"Some people think so. If I'm going to cleanse the spectral entity, I have to know what I'm dealing with."

"Count me out." Debbie stood and went back to her bed, dropping onto the mattress and picking up the unicorn.

"I understand." Tatyana glanced over at the desk. "Are you a writer?"

"I want to be. How did you know?"

Tatyana picked up a book from the blotter on writing fiction. "What do you usually write about?"

"Besides my journal, mostly short romance stories."

"Are you working on a horror novel now?"

"After what happened the other night, yes."

"Wouldn't it be great research for your book to witness a professional ghost hunter track down an evil entity?"

"You're good." Debbie smirked. "Wouldn't I be in danger?"

"I can make sure no harm will come to you and Alison. If anyone is in danger, it'll be me."

"Then count me in."

Tatyana turned to Alison. "Is that okay with you?"

"It's fine with me. The trick will be convincing Mrs. Delillo."

"Don't worry about mom. I can handle her."

"Then it's settled," said Tatyana. "Alison will pick you up tonight at two-thirty."

CHAPTER ELEVEN

8 June 1862
Salem Village

THE HUMIDITY HUNG heavily in the air, overpowering and oppressive, much like the hatred and fear infiltrating every corner of this once peaceful village. It was only noon and would become even more unbearable as the day wore on. That didn't stop most villagers from turning out and lining the streets around Salem Town Jail. For a society that shunned entertainment and pageantry, that gathered only to exalt and worship the Lord God, today was a special occasion, one that allowed them to indulge in what would otherwise be a sin, only now cloaked in a shroud of acceptability.

Today Bridget Bishop would be hanged as a witch.

The entire affair both disgusted and terrified Eliza. Disgust because they were hanging an innocent woman based solely on her checkered past and the dislike felt toward her by the hypocritically righteous Puritans. Terrified because the proceedings were spiraling out of control, ensnaring even more innocents in its insidious web.

Eliza knew her fate would be no better, and more than likely far worse, if they discovered her secret. Eliza feared she was witnessing her future.

Excitement surged through the crowd. Sheriff George Corwin led Bridget Bishop from the jail and to a cart that sat out front. The woman appeared physically haggard and spiritually broken after months of confinement in a cell not fit for cattle. Nor did it help that she had endured continued questioning about her association with witchcraft in which the only acceptable answer was a confession of guilt, a crime she had not committed and refused to admit to. The sheriff assisted her into the back of the cart and tied her hands to the upright support. With the prisoner secured, he stepped off, mounted his horse, and led the way. The cart lumbered down Prison Lane flanked on either side by guards on foot and mounted constables.

A bystander masked by the anonymity of the crowd screamed, "Witch!"

The mantra spread through the street like the water from a river that had broken its banks. The Puritan code of forgiveness gave way to mass hysteria. Dozens of people cried out, belittling the woman, labeling her as a consort of the Devil, and condemning her to damnation. Occasionally, someone summoned the courage to throw a rotten piece of fruit or small stone, further adding to the poor woman's indignity. As Corwin led the cart to the southwest, the crowd followed, a morbid procession excited to witness the grim outcome.

Eliza fell in with them, horrified yet compelled to see this injustice through until the end.

Since no one had even been put to death in Salem Village, a makeshift execution spot had been erected in a pasture southwest of the village. Turning off Prison Lane, the procession headed along the road leading to Salem Village and, beyond that, Andover. Here the North River took a sharp bend to the north, connecting with a stream that flowed from the southern heights into a salty marsh area. Once the procession crossed the causeway over the stream and the bridge across the river, it turned left off the main road and followed a dirt track a ledge above the marsh. Sheriff Corwin stopped. The crowd gathered around.

Among them were some of Bridget Bishop's accusers, still putting on their pathetic little charade even as a woman they had condemned to the gallows faced her last moments of life.

Eliza felt nausea rising from the pit of her stomach, only wishing she could be there to watch these childish manipulators reap what they had sowed.

Corwin climbed into the cart, untied the prisoner, then bound her hands behind her back. Helping Bridget Bishop onto the ground, the sheriff led her to a line of trees at the edge of the ledge where everyone would be able to witness her punishment. One of the trees had a ladder leaning against a thick, low-lying branch. A noose dangled from the bough. As the sheriff tied her legs together and wrapped rope around her dress, a feeble attempt at preserving the condemned women's dignity, Bridget Bishop pleaded her case one final time.

"I swear to you, on the Holy Bible and as God the Almighty as my witness, that I am a woman pure of heart and have never dabbled in witchcraft."

An older woman dressed in shabby clothes admonished, "You had your chance to make your peace with God."

One of the accusers dropped to her knees, clutched her throat, and choked. She pointed an accusatory finger at Bridget Bishop. Another accuser comforted her choking friend as a second turned to the crowd.

"See. Even in her last moments, she torments us. Is that not proof enough of her guilt?"

Cries of "witch" and "hang her" echoed from the crowd.

Behind Eliza, a well-dressed man in his thirties whom she did not recognize – probably someone from Salem Town here to witness the hanging – yelled out, "Get on with it."

Beside Eliza, a girl barely eight years old shielded her eyes from the horror about to be perpetrated. Her mother grabbed her hands and forced them by her side. "You watch what's about to take place. This is what happens when you stray from God."

Only one person prayed for the poor woman's soul, a visiting minister from Beverly who bowed his head and whispered a prayer.

With the prisoner properly bound, the sheriff placed a hood over Bridget Bishop's head. She ceased the protestations of her innocence and recited the Lord's Prayer, the words frenzied by the terror overwhelming her. As one of the constables held the ladder, two others assisted the prisoner up the rungs, making sure she was up high enough to have her neck broken in the fall. One of them took the noose and placed it around Bridget Bishop's neck. Both climbed down and stepped a safe distance away.

Sheriff Corwin approached the ladder and stood beside it.

"Bridget Oliver Bishop, for the crime of witchcraft and consorting with the Devil, I sentence thee to be hanged by the neck until you are dead. May God bless your soul."

With that, Corwin pushed the prisoner off the ladder.

Her body dropped, stopping only when the noose tightened. Yet the fall had not broken her neck instantly as intended. The noose tightened around her neck, strangling the poor woman. She kicked and twisted. Above her head, the bough audibly strained under the pressure.

Around Eliza, the crowd became silent. No one was prepared for the nightmare they witnessed. Even the accusers ceased their melodramatic accusations, whether from guilt over the death they had initiated or as part of the plot to ensure the crowd believed their sordid tale. No one would ever know. The jaunting died more rapidly than the prisoner did.

After a few minutes, Bridget Bishop's feet stopped kicking. Her body went limp, the carcass now swinging slowly back and forth at the end of the rope.

Eliza closed her eyes. An innocent life had been taken.

Slowly and silently, the crowd dispersed and headed back to Salem Village, much more quiet and solemn than on the journey up. Corwin ordered two men to remove the ladder and place it in the cart, then they departed. The sheriff left the body of the executed to dangle from the tree so it would be visible from the road, a warning to everyone that those who defied the will of God and consorted with the Devil would pay the ultimate price for their sins.

Eliza left before Corwin and his people.

She returned late in the afternoon of the next day. Someone had come by that morning and cut down the deceased. Eliza searched the area until she eventually found the body, which had been tossed off the ledge into the rocky crevice below. Whoever had disposed of her saw fit to cover the woman's grave with a few handfuls of dirt.

Bridget Bishop had been treated with the same lack of respect in death as she had been during her condemnation.

Eliza feared this would only be the beginning of the nightmare.

CHAPTER TWELVE

NICK WAITED FOR Tatyana when she returned to her hotel room. He lay on Nostradamus' bed watching television, his back inclined on the headboard and his ankles crossed. The dog curled up asleep beside him, snoring loudly. She stepped inside, an expression of surprise on her face.

"I didn't expect to find you here." Tatyana slid off her jacket and draped it over the back of a chair. She crossed over to the bathroom and paused, staring at the TV. "How did you turn it on?"

Nick lifted his right hand and wiggled his forefinger. "I've learned to channel my spectral energy so my finger can become corporeal. It gives me the ability to turn on electronics and change channels on the remote."

"Really?" Tatyana stepped into the bathroom and washed her hands.

"Do you want me to poke you with my finger to show you?"

"Do you want to see if a spirit's finger can be broken?"

"I'll pass." Nick chuckled and browsed through the channels. "Can I ask you something?"

"Sure."

"None of this makes sense. Why are SyFy Channel showing action films, National Geographics showing history documentaries, and The History Channel showing... whatever it is they're showing?"

Tatyana stood in the center of the doorway, drying her hands on a towel. "That's right. You died before the age of television. Trust me. You're not missing much."

"I know. But *Ancient Aliens*? Do people believe that crap?"

"Have you found the paranormal shows yet?"

Nick's eyes widened. "You mean like what we do?"

Tatyana nodded.

"Please tell me you're joking."

"I'm not. It's a riot. Most are young guys who hunt ghosts in old castles and scream at the slightest sound. They'd piss themselves if they encountered the spirits we have."

Nick shook his head. "I feel so out of place in this time."

"You'll get used to it after a while." Tatyana exited the bathroom, shut off the light, and crossed over to her bed. She slipped off her heels and rolled onto the mattress. "Would you mind turning off the television? I want to catch some sleep. We're going back to Pioneer Village tonight with Debbie to see if we can contact the spirit that attacked them."

"No problem." Nick pressed the off button on the remote. "Would you mind if I use your computer? I want to look up things I saw on television that made me curious."

"Do you know how to use it?"

"I've watched you enough times."

"You tend to watch a lot of things I do." Tatyana grinned and pulled the covers over her. "Would you wake me at eight?"

"Of course."

Tatyana fell asleep within minutes, joining Nostradamus in the snoring.

Nick went over to the desk, sat down, and called up the Internet. He had seen a few documentaries about World War II and the post-war era that intrigued him, so he started his search there. He found a photograph of the destroyer he had served on, which brought back pleasant memories. Reading the history of the war fascinated him. There were so many things he had not been aware of while in the Pacific. And though the stories about the atrocities committed by the Germans and Japanese disgusted him, he had to admit he was not surprised considering what he had observed.

Next, he delved into the Cold War. The nuclear arms race shocked him. Nick remembered being grateful for the atomic bombs dropped on Hiroshima and Nagasaki. They ended the war quickly and saved millions of lives. To read that the superpowers then created enough nuclear weapons to destroy the world several times over boggled his mind. And so many wars. Korea. Vietnam. The Cuban Missile Crisis. The Arab-Israeli conflicts. The collapse of the Soviet Union. Terrorism. Two wars in Iraq and one in Afghanistan. He thought World War II had been brutal. Amazingly, the world survived those years.

Nick then researched the Vietnam protests and the civil rights movement. As a soldier who had put his life on the line for his country, the protests infuriated him, though he could understand their frustration over the way the government handled the conflict. The civil rights movement was riveting. He recalled having black sailors in the Navy, but they had all been consigned to galley duty and never saw combat.

One topic he kept coming upon piqued his interest – the sexual revolution. Nick double-checked to make certain Tatyana was still asleep before typing the term into the search engine. Damn, he thought television was fun. The loosening of society's sexual restriction was startling. And he would still have been old enough to take part. He was sorry he missed out on that.

Nick typed sex into the search engine, stunned by the results. There were so many sites devoted only to sex. He spent the next hour going through them until it overwhelmed him. MILFs. GILFs. TILFs. Gangbangs. Blowbangs. Amateur videos. Interracial. And some bizarre shit from Germany and Japan. And he thought the stuff his shipmates got involved in on shore leave was crazy? These made their antics seem like a Boy Scout outing.

He closed the lid of Tatyana's laptop and closed his eyes,

trying to push the mental images from his mind. Easier said than done. A lot had changed in the past eighty years. It would take Nick some time to get used to it all.

CHAPTER THIRTEEN

TATYANA PULLED HER car into one of the parking spaces in the lot outside of Pioneer Village and shut off the engine. A Salem Police squad car sat three spaces away. The wooden wall surrounding the site stood in the dark in front of them and, beyond it, the trees surrounding the village from view. The only light came from the few neon streetlamps located around the lot. This portion of the park appeared ominous, a sensation heightened by her knowledge that something existed on the other side of the fence.

"I don't like this place," said Nick from the passenger's seat. "There's a malevolent spirit in there."

"Do you know what?"

"No." Nick met her gaze. "But it's evil."

The sound of a car door opening came from her left. The Salem Police officer approached. Alissa rolled down the window. Nostradamus jumped up from the back seat and shoved his head past her headrest and out the open window, his tail wagging and his tongue hanging out of his mouth. The officer wore a stern expression.

"May I help you?"

"I'm Tatyana Reynolds. I'm waiting for Alison Bechtel."

The officer's demeanor changed. He smiled and tipped his hat. "I was told to expect you. Miss Bechtel should be here shortly."

Alissa checked the clock on her dashboard. It read 2:37.

"I'm early."

"No problem, ma'am."

Nostradamus whined, demanding attention. The officer stepped forward and held out the top of his right hand. Nostradamus licked it. The officer reached up and scratched the dog's head.

"Who's a good boy?"

Nostradamus answered with a bark.

"Have a good night." The officer tipped his hat again and strolled back to his squad car.

"You love a man in uniform," teased Nick.

"You're in uniform, and I barely tolerate you," she jibed back.

"Ouch," Nick replied jokingly. "I'm going to go on ahead and scout out the area. See you inside."

"Okay, but please don't—"

Nick disappeared, becoming a mist that flowed through the roof.

Dammit, thought Tatyana. *I hate it when he does that.*

Nostradamus barked.

A few minutes later, Alison's car entered the lot and parked beside Tatyana. Alison climbed out. She wore casual street clothes with a denim jacket and a pair of designer boots. If she had any apprehension about tonight, it did not show. Debbie exited from the passenger's side, the fear evident in her eyes. She stared at Pioneer Village, frozen in place, obviously regretting her decision to return.

Tatyana walked over to the teenager. "Are you sure you want to do this?"

"Hell, no. I'm scared to death." Debbie shifted her stance and made eye contact with Tatyana. "Can you promise me that if I go through with this, you can prevent that... thing... from going after others?"

"Yes."

Debbie nodded. "Then let's do this."

As Alison chatted with the police officer, Tatyana removed a knapsack from the trunk that she slung over her left shoulder.

She opened the rear passenger door. Nostradamus bounced around the back seat. Attaching the leash to his chest harness, she let him out and was pulled onto the grass so the dog could relieve himself.

Alison joined them. "John's going to stay out here and make sure no one disturbs us. He gave me this." She held a whistle by the chain then slipped it into her jacket pocket. "I'm to use it if we get into trouble. We won't need it, will we?"

"Of course not," Tatyana lied. It wasn't a lie. If the situation reached a point that they needed to call in the police, by then it would probably be too late.

Alison led the way to the gate. She stopped, withdrew a key from her pocket, and inserted it into the lock.

"How did you sneak in?" Alison asked Debbie.

The teenager hesitated. "We had a spare key."

"Twenty to one Tom's brother made it when he worked here." Alison swung open the twin gates and ushered the others inside. As they entered, each switched on their flashlights.

"You lead the way," Tatyana suggested to Debbie. "And tell us everything that happened."

Debbie swallowed hard and headed inside, crossing the small footbridge and stopping in front of the tourist shop. "We spent a few minutes here goofing around. Cindy wanted a picture of her in the stocks."

"Did you do anything insulting?" asked Alison.

"No, but we weren't on our best behavior."

"Is this where you began drinking?" asked Tatyana.

Debbie shook her head. "The others started in the parking lot. I didn't drink anything that night. I kept urging them to leave."

"I assume they ignored you?"

Debbie nodded and lowered her head.

"Where did you go next?"

Debbie pointed to the footbridge down the path to their right. "That way."

A few minutes later, they arrived in front of the Governor's Mansion. A run-down fence surrounded the two-story wooden structure. Directly across from it sat a garden enclosed by the same old-style fence and two modern benches by the gate. "This is where we were when the ghost appeared. We were... they were drinking. It came after us as we were leaving."

"Where did the spirit first appear?"

Debbie pointed to the mansion. "From inside there."

Tatyana left Nostradamus with the others, walked over to the house, and placed her right hand on the door. She felt a strong aura pulsing through the wood. This spirit was powerful.

Nick materialized beside her. "This is definitely where it resides. I can sense it."

"I can feel it myself," she whispered. "Who does it belong to?"

"I have no idea. I tried talking to it, but it refuses to acknowledge me. I pissed it off. Strong emotions emanate from this spirit."

"Anger?"

"Rage." Nick glanced over at Tatyana. "Be careful with this one."

"Who are you talking to?" Alison called out.

"Myself." Tatyana rejoined the group. "What did you do while you were here?"

"Nothing much. Mostly drinking. John thought this was the place where they burned the witches."

"No one accused of witchcraft was burned," corrected Alison. "They were all hanged at Gallows Hill."

"That's what Tom told us."

"Did anyone do anything to provoke the spirit?" Alison asked.

"No. We didn't even know it was here. They drank for a while and then we headed.... Shit. I just remembered." Debbie's eyes widened. "As we were leaving, John picked up a twig with three branches, lit it, and called it a witch on fire.

That's when the ghost appeared."

"Interesting."

Nick maneuvered into Tatyana's line of sight. "That's what set it off. I just felt a spike in its rage."

Tatyana placed Nostradamus' leash on the ground beside her. The dog laid down. She set her knapsack on the bench and unzipped it. Removing a cylindrical cardboard container of salt, she poured out a ring six feet in diameter in front of the garden. Next, she withdrew four sage candles and lay them on the salt circle at each of the four compass points.

"Your job is to protect this spot, as well as Alison and Debbie, from all spirits, benign and malevolent, but particularly the spirit present in this mansion. I know you'll do as I ask."

"What are you doing?" asked Alison.

"She's making a circle of salt to protect us when she summons the ghost," answered Debbie.

Alison stared at her. "You told us you didn't dabble in the occult."

"I don't. But I've seen enough horror movies to figure out what she's doing."

"Debbie's right." Tatyana removed six Selenite crystals from the knapsack. She placed four on the salt circle between the candles.

"Your job is to assist the salt circle in protecting Alison and Debbie from all spirits, benign and malevolent, but particularly the spirit present in this mansion. I know you'll do as I ask."

Tatyana handed one crystal each to Alison and Debbie. Debbie turned it over in her hand. "What are these?"

"Selenite crystals. It emits a vibration that generates positive energy and helps ward off evil spirits."

"Is there any danger?" Alison asked nervously.

"You're welcome to stay out here with me?"

"No thanks."

"Will you be okay?" asked Debbie.

"I've done this before. I'll be fine." *At least, I hope so,*

Tatyana added mentally.

She motioned to the center of the salt circle. "You two stand in there."

Alison and Debbie complied. Both women appeared nervous, the former hiding it better than the teenager. Tatyana lit the sage candles and stood to the side.

"Whatever happens, don't leave that circle unless I tell you to."

"Don't worry," said Alison. "We won't."

Tatyana moved to the left of the circle and stood by Nostradamus. Nick positioned himself several yards to her left.

"I'm calling on the spirit who resides in the mansion. I want to talk with you."

She received no response. Tatyana sensed no change in the spectral aura.

"She's ignoring you," said Nick.

"To the spirit who resides here, please contact me. I mean you no harm. I only wish to talk with you."

Still nothing.

Tatyana walked around the grounds, finally picking up a twig with three branches extending from one end. She gave it to Debbie along with a box of matches.

"I want you to light this like John did the last time you were here."

"Are you crazy?" The teenager stepped back. "That'll piss her off again."

"I'm hoping it does. I need to get her attention."

Debbie hesitated.

"Please. It's the only way to contact her."

"You promise nothing will happen to me?"

"Yes, as long as you stay inside the circle."

Reluctantly, Debbie took the items. Striking a match, she held it to the end of the branches until they caught fire. When the top of the twig burned, she held it in front of her.

"Look at me. I'm a witch on fire. Argh."

Tatyana winced as the spectral aura spiked. She sensed rage emanating from the mansion.

Nostradamus jumped to his feet and stared at the mansion, growling.

Nick took a step back and pointed to the second floor. "Shit."

A luminescent glow appeared in the room on the left. As they watched, it made its way to the stairwell and descended to the first floor, then emerged through the wood of the closed door. The light flowed across the courtyard, forming into the spectral image of a young woman in her mid-twenties. As it drew closer to the salt circle, the white glow darkened, taking on a harsh, yellowish hue. Tatyana expected to see the image of a human. Instead, this spirit had scraggily hair, charred and blistered skin, and a mouth distorted with blackened teeth. Upon seeing Debbie holding the twig, it surged forward and lunged at the salt circle, stopping at its edge and bellowing a howl, half fury and half agony.

Debbie screamed and dropped the twig.

"You taunt me, bitch." The spectral image studied her for a moment. Its eyes widened and its expression grew furious. "I remember you. You were one of those here the other night making fun of me. I told you I would make you suffer if you returned."

"Enough!" yelled Tatyana. "Leave her alone. I'm the one who asked her to do that."

The spirit spun around to face Tatyana. "Apparently, you don't value your life."

"I do, as much as I value yours."

"Then why do something so foolhardy?"

"It was the only way to get you to talk to me."

Nostradamus' ears went back and his tail folded under his body. He glared at the spirit and growled.

"Restrain your hound or I'll strike it dead."

Nick yelled out," She's capable of doing it."

Tatyana crouched down and picked up the leash, holding the dog close to her side.

The spirit glided over to Tatyana and studied her for several seconds. "You have some of the same abilities as me."

"You're also a Necroscope?"

"Among other things. What do you want with me?"

"Only to talk. I'm Tatyana Reynolds. What's your name?"

The spirit refused to answer.

"It'll be a lot easier if I knew your name."

The spirit hesitated. "I am Eliza."

"Why are you here?"

"Not of my own free will." Her voice dripped with anger, but not directed toward anyone present. "I was condemned to be bound to this place for all eternity."

"Why?"

Eliza did not respond.

"What do you want?" asked Tatyana. "Revenge?"

"Petty mortal," Eliza screamed. "What good would revenge do me? My tormenters are long since dead."

"Then what do you want?"

Again, Eliza did not answer.

"I can't help you if you don't tell me how."

"Why do you want to help me?"

"You know the answer to that. I can feel you in my soul. Something terrible happened to you. Something unimaginable. You were wronged."

Eliza stared at Tatyana, sympathy replacing some of the rage in her eyes.

"Please tell me what happened."

"I played with fire and I got burned." Eliza laughed sardonically.

"What happened to you?"

"You'll have to figure that out on your own."

"What do you want?"

"Recognition and justice." Eliza sneered. "Is that too much

to ask for?"

"It's not. But I can't help you release yourself from this torment if I don't know what happened."

"Behind you," warned Nick.

A figure approached from the tourist center. He carried a flashlight. As he drew closer, she recognized him as John, the Salem Police officer from out front.

"I heard someone scream. Is everyone all—" His beam fell on the spectral image of Eliza. "What's going on here?"

"We're fine, sheriff," Tatyana called out, using the wrong title for John.

"Sheriff?" Rage filled Eliza's eyes. She shot across the compound, heading directly for the officer.

John withdrew his service weapon and aimed but did not fire, realizing the three women were in his line of sight. Eliza knocked the gun out of his hand. Wrapping both hands around John's neck, she lifted him off the ground and began strangling him. He choked for air.

Alison left the salt circle and ran over to help John, abandoning Debbie.

"Don't leave me!" the teenager yelled.

"Nick. Nostradamus. Protect Debbie." Tatyana went after Alison.

The dog ran into the circle and pressed himself against Debbie's leg. Nick ran to the outer edge and materialized so Debbie could see him. She screamed again.

"Don't worry," said Nick. "I'm with Tatyana. I'll protect you."

John's complexion had already turned blue when Alison reached him. She clasped both hands together, raised her arms, and swung down against Eliza's head. Her hands passed through the spirit. For a moment, Alison froze, an expression of terror on her face. Still choking John in her right hand, Eliza struck out with her left, catching Alison across the left temple. Alison dropped to the dirt, stunned.

Tatyana raced up. "What are you doing?"

"The constable must die!"

"I demand you leave them alone."

Eliza glared at her, still holding John in the air with one hand. "No."

"In the name of God, the Father, and the Almighty, I demand you release this man and return to your mansion."

Eliza dropped John. He fell to the ground, gasping for air. She moved closer to Tatyana, who backed away.

"I'm not your typical spirit wandering this realm who you can easily dispatch. I was bound here and cannot leave."

"I demand that you return to your mansion."

Eliza reached out and ran her hand down Tatyana's cheek, creating four three-inch-long marks. Tatyana yelped from pain.

"Your God is no match for me. I am far more powerful." Eliza stepped back. "You are free to go. All except the girl. She defied my orders never to return her and must pay for her defiance."

Eliza floated back to the salt circle. Debbie screamed at the top of her lungs.

Tatyana raced over to John. He sat up, his breathing belabored, but he would live. "Can you walk?"

"What is that thing?"

"Can you walk?" she yelled.

"Yes."

"Get Alison out of here."

"What about the girl?"

"I'll take care of her. Now go while you can."

John climbed to his feet and helped Alison up. Together, the two limped back to the parking lot.

Tatyana ran after Eliza.

"Help me!" Debbie screamed.

Nick placed himself between Eliza and Debbie. "Leave the girl alone."

"She must be punished for her insolence."

Nostradamus barked. Debbie grabbed his leash and held him back.

Eliza glared at the dog. Nostradamus whimpered and ran behind Debbie for protection.

Nick moved closer to Eliza. "Step away now or you'll have to deal with me."

Eliza laughed, the hysterical sound of someone who has gone insane. She shot out her left hand toward him. Nick's image dissolved into a spectral mist. Eliza blew on him, blowing away the mist.

Tatyana paused long enough to pull out of her knapsack a small bottle emblazoned with a cross and charged Eliza. "Damn you."

"You're three hundred years too late." Eliza turned to face the new threat.

Tatyana flicked the bottle at her. A stream of Holy Water flew out of the opening, splashing Eliza across the face. The spirit howled in agony. Tatyana raised the bottle above Eliza's head and emptied the contents onto her. Eliza shrieked and thrashed about. Her corporeal form broke down into a white mist that withdrew inside the mansion.

Tatyana grabbed Debbie's hand. The front of the teenager's jeans was soaked in urine. "Let's go."

The two of them ran for the exit, Tatyana grabbing her knapsack as they passed by. Nostradamus ran ahead of them, whimpering and checking behind him every few seconds to ensure his mistress was safe. They did not stop until they reached their cars.

As Tatyana gasped to catch her breath, Debbie slapped her across the face, striking the cheek not scratched.

"You goddamn bitch. You nearly got me killed."

"I'm sorry."

"Bullshit. You promised to protect me." Debbie moved closer and pounded her fists against Tatyana's chest, the intensity of the blows decreasing until the teenager broke down in tears and rested her head against Tatyana.

She hugged Debbie tight. "It's okay. You're safe now."

The teenager sobbed.

Alison came over and gently placed her hands on Debbie's shoulders. "Get in the car, hon. I'll take you home."

Debbie broke her grip. Alison helped her into the passenger side. Once she closed the door, she returned to Tatyana.

"That was terrifying," said Alison.

"I've never experienced anything that bad."

"We'll talk in the morning." I'll drop by your room around nine. Go back to your hotel and rest. We all need to detox after what happened."

Alison went back to her car and drove away. John sat in his squad car with the windows rolled up, focusing on Tatyana with a look that expressed anger, fear, and confusion. It pained Tatyana to think how many people had been hurt tonight because of her.

Tatyana helped Nostradamus climb into the front seat and then headed back to the Hawthorne Inn.

CHAPTER FOURTEEN

19 July 1692
Salem Village

ELIZA AND OTHER villagers gathered outside Salem Jail, waiting for the inevitable. Four people already stood in the wooden cart out front, their hands bound. The atmosphere should be somber, but it was not. The crowd seemed excited. Evil gripped Salem Village to the point that, even on a day as dark as this, the locals greeted it as if it were a celebration. Women abandoned their chores and men left their fields untended, bringing their children to witness the proceedings.

Fear and stupidity had become the norm. After a twenty-six-day hiatus, the Court of Oyer and Terminus resumed. Five more innocent lives were found guilty and sentenced to the gallows, among them Rebecca Nurse. Her trial had been a travesty.

Many of the villagers pleaded on Rebecca's behalf, some courageously condemning their accusers for their actions. At first, it seemed to work because the jury found Rebecca not guilty. Then the judge intervened, pressuring the jury that the evidence against the accused was insurmountable. The jury retracted its verdict and declared Rebecca guilty of witchcraft. Petitions to the governor convinced him to pardon the woman until the outcry caused him to revoke the decree. Two weeks ago, the church excommunicated Rebecca, condemning her soul to eternal damnation.

Rebecca Nurse, Sarah Martin, Elizabeth Howe, Sarah Good, and Sarah Wildes were about to be hanged.

Sheriff Corwin led Rebecca Nurse out of the jail building, her hands tied, and helped her into the cart. Some of the villagers quietly told those nearby that it was about time justice would be done and, maybe, this would all be over soon. Some prayed, either to themselves or muttering under their breath to God. Eliza heard none of this. She closed her eyes and begged that the souls of the five people before her would forgive her cowardice.

Corwin led the cart away, surrounded by guards, and made his way through the dusty streets toward Gallows Hill. The crowd followed the procession, eerily quiet.

When they arrived at their destination, one of the deputies maneuvered the cart beneath the bough of a large tree. The deputies had slung five ropes had over the bough. The guards climbed onto the cart, pulling the nooses over the heads of the accused and tightening them.

Reverend Nicholas Noyes, the same man of the cloth who had excommunicated Rebecca a few weeks ago, stepped in front of the condemned.

"I offer you one last chance at redemption. Confess to being witches and maybe the Heavenly Father will spare your souls."

"I am not a witch," said Sarah Good.

"Still thy tongue. I know you are a witch."

"You are a liar," spat Sarah. "I am no more a witch than you are a wizard. If you take my life, God will give you enough to drink."

"Enough," yelled Noyes.

As the reverend walked away, Corwin gave the signal. One of the deputies slapped the horse, causing it to move forward. The five condemned dropped off the rear of the cart and dangled. Their bodies twitched and struggled as life was slowly choke out of them. One by one, the bodies stopped their dances of death until the five corpses hung motionless, swaying in the wind. The deputies took down each body and dragged them over to the ravine by the side of the hill to be thrown in without a second thought or final blessing. The deputies threw some rocks and dirt over them, the only burial they would have.

Slowly the villagers filed away, heading home to complete the mundanity of their chores. All but Eliza. She stayed behind, fighting back the tears. To show emotion over their deaths would serve only to add herself to the list of accused. She blamed herself for these executions, as she knew she would blame those of anyone condemned to die in the future. One thought kept racing through her mind.

What have I done?

CHAPTER FIFTEEN

TATYANA STARED AT her image in the mirror. The four scratches across her left cheek where Eliza had attacked her were red and enflamed. It appeared like she had an encounter with a wild animal, which wasn't far from the truth. Thankfully, the bitch had not broken skin. Though horrible now, in time they would heal.

Nostradamus issued a happy bark from the other room, followed a moment later by Nick's voice.

"Are you here?"

Tatyana raced out of the bathroom to find Nick standing by the bed, petting Nostradamus.

He smiled. "It's good to see—"

She wrapped her arms around Nick. The hug passed through him.

Nick chuckled. "What's that for?"

"I was worried something bad had happened after Eliza…." Tatyana could not find the right words.

"All she did was send me to another location. I would have come back sooner, but whatever power she used disoriented my ability to locate you."

Tatyana felt relieved her friend had returned. "I'm glad you're okay."

"You're not." Nick studied the scratches on her face. "She got you pretty bad last night."

"These?" Tatyana self-consciously raised her hand to her face. "They'll heal."

"Did you get Debbie out?"

"Yes. I had to douse Eliza with holy water which distracted her enough so we could get away."

"How are the others?"

"Fine, I guess. We all went our separate ways once we reached the parking lot. I came back here but barely slept. I'm exhausted and—"

The ringing of her cell phone interrupted Tatyana. Alison was calling. She hit the accept button.

"I'm in the lobby. Can I come up?"

"Sure. The door is unlocked."

"See you in a bit."

Tatyana ended the connection.

"Do you want me to leave?" asked Nick.

"No."

A few minutes later, the door to the room opened and Alison stepped in, closing it behind her. She wore the same clothes she had on the night before. Tatyana's eyes were drawn to a large bruise on the woman's left cheek. It had swollen and turned red. The black and blue had already formed around the center. In a few days, Alison would look like she had been in a fight.

"Eliza got you bad," Tatyana said sympathetically.

"Not as bad as you. Did she draw blood?"

"Thank God, no." Tatyana motioned to the chair by the desk. "Would you like to sit?"

"I'd love to, but I won't be staying long. I haven't been home since what happened at Pioneer Village."

"How are Debbie and John?"

"They're fine." Alison rolled her eyes and shook her head. "Of course, Debbie was terrified after what happened. When I brought her home, her mother yelled at me for half an hour and told me how irresponsible I am."

"That's my fault," admitted Tatyana.

"Mine, too. I agreed to let Debbie come with us. Anyways, Mrs. Delillo threatened to go to the media with what happened."

"Will she?"

"No. I finally convinced her that doing so would only place Debbie in the spotlight, which neither of us wanted."

"Good. The last thing we want is glory seekers and amateur ghost hunters running around the village."

Alison rolled her eyes. "God forbid. That would be a public relations nightmare."

"What about John?"

"He's fine. Some bad bruising on his neck but no internal injuries. Though that poses another set of problems."

"How so?"

Alison sighed and sat on the edge of the bed closest to the door. "He refuses to write up a report about last night, afraid they'll either fire him or lock him up in the nuthouse. His word, not mine. The chief is yelling at the mayor, wanting to know what happened, and the mayor is yelling at me, wanting to know why you haven't exorcised this thing yet. Don't worry. I told the mayor about what happened."

"Did he believe you?"

Alison shrugged. "I think so. I told him this was much worse than we imagined and we needed more time. He agreed to give you two more days."

"Then what?"

"He'll tell me to figure it out."

An awkward silence followed, broken by Tatyana asking, "Do you have faith in me?"

"To be honest, I was skeptical about this whole evil spirit at Pioneer Village from the start. I thought the kids were pulling a prank. That all changed last night. In answer to your question, yes, if anyone is going to get rid of that thing, I think I'll be you."

From behind Alison, Nick said, "We still have no clue who Eliza is and why she's bound to that area."

Tatyana met his gaze. "That's true."

Alison glanced over her shoulder, seeing nothing but empty space, then leaned closer to Tatyana. "Do you have a ghost companion?"

"Why do you ask?"

"For one thing, you're talking to someone I can't see, so you're either chatting with a ghost or you're crazy, and I'm praying it's not the latter. Plus, Debbie told me about how a ghost who said he was a friend of yours protected her from Eliza."

"I do," Tatyana confessed. "His name is Nick. He accompanies me on my trips. He probably saved Debbie's life last night. Do you want to meet him?"

"No." Alison stood and raised her hands, then looked in his general direction. "No offense, Nick. I've already seen way too much for my mind to process."

Nick laughed.

"Nick was saying to me that we have no idea who Eliza is and why she's here."

"That's the other reason I'm here." Alison removed a business card from her wallet and handed it to Tatyana. "I arranged an interview with you this morning with Denholm Goss. He's the educational director at the Peabody Essex Institute just down the street and an expert on the Salem Witch Trials. He'll answer any questions you have about that period. The time of the appointment is on the back."

"Will you be joining me?"

"Hell, no. The mayor told me not to come into work until this bruise heals. He doesn't want any attention drawn to what's going on. I'm heading home to take a hot shower, drink a few Mimosas, and sleep. If I can sleep after last night." Alison exited, pausing at the door. "Don't hesitate to call me if you need anything. If I don't answer, leave a voice mail. Good luck."

Nick stared after Alison as she left. "I don't know whether I should be offended or not," he joked. "I may be a spirit, but

I'm still charming and handsome."

Tatyana smirked. "She's smart. You take getting used to."

"What now?"

"My meeting in a little over an hour. I'm going to have breakfast and take Nostradamus for a walk."

CHAPTER SIXTEEN

T ATYANA EXITED THE Hawthorne Inn. The Peabody Essex Institute sat across the road from the hotel. She crossed with the traffic signal and proceeded along Essex Street. The institute was the largest and most popular tourist attraction in Salem, containing museum pieces and historical documents encompassing its history since its founding in 1626. It curated residences from the early 17th to mid-19th centuries across Salem. Everything about the city's maritime, social, political, and literary history was contained here, including the documents dating back to the infamous witch trials. In a few minutes, she would meet Denholm Goss, the director of education at the Peabody Essex Institute, Salem's most eminent scholar on that infamous period and the man who had studied the documentation from the proceedings.

The central location of the institute was located at 144 Essex Street. It occupied two buildings. The mansion on the right, a three-story structure designed in the style typical of homes in the 1850s but with Italianate details, once belonged to John Tucker Daland, one of the city's more prominent maritime merchants. The Plummer House, the two-story building on the left built around the same time, once housed a private library. She entered.

The foyer was both elegant and massive. The grand staircase sat along the right wall and extended to the exhibit rooms on the second floor and the offices on the third. The rooms along the left had been converted into a gift shop and a conference hall, each tastefully designed to match the rest of the first floor. A dozen people milled about, waiting for the tour of the various residences on the site.

Tatyana crossed over to the receptionist's counter. A young woman in a tasteful sundress and the nametag on her white sweater that read Wendy looked up and smiled.

"Are you here for the tour? You're just in time. It's beginning in a few minutes."

"No. I have an appointment with Denholm Goss."

"You must be Tatyana."

"I am."

"I'll let him know you're here. Please feel free to look around."

Tatyana wandered over to the gift shop and browsed through the rack of postcards on display.

The elevator at the rear of the foyer pinged. Tatyana thought it might be Denholm. Instead, a young woman stepped out. She was tall, slender, attractive, and of college age. She checked in with Wendy then headed over to the group.

"Good morning. I'm Julie. I'm your tour guide." She checked each person for their tickets as she went through the mantra of rules. Photography was allowed, touching items in the houses was not. No food or beverages were allowed inside the homes. Smoking was prohibited on the property. With that out of the way, Julie led them to the rear exit. "Our first stop this morning will be the John Ward House."

Tatyana grinned. To be young and back in college as a student with her entire life ahead of her. Those were carefree days. And though embarrassed now by how she partied in those days, a part of her missed having no responsibilities. It also reminded her she needed to concentrate more on her studies. At this rate, she would never complete her Ph.D.

A young man came down the stairs wearing jeans and a dress shirt. She figured him to be in his mid- to late thirties. He was clean-shaven with dark blonde hair coiffured into a wave. A pair of rectangular eyeglasses with no frame sat on his nose.

Confidence exuded from him. Tatyana tried not to stare. If she had time to date and if she lived closer, she might....

Oh, shit. Tatyana went back to scanning the postcards, feeling self-conscious. He headed toward her. He must have spotted her checking him out.

He walked up to her. "Are you Tatyana?"

"How do you know my name?" she asked awkwardly.

"I'm Denholm Goss." A pleasant smile pierced his lips. He held out his hand. "It's a pleasure to meet you."

Tatyana took his hand. It felt warm and soft. "The pleasure is mine."

"Let's go to my office where we can talk in private. Do you want to take the stairs or the elevator?"

"The stairs. I can always use the exercise."

Denholm led her up to the third floor. "Have you been in Salem long?"

"Only two days. I haven't seen much of the city."

"That's too bad. Salem is such a beautiful city. Are you into history?"

"I'm getting my doctorate in history."

"Where?"

"At Dartmouth."

"That's a great campus," said Denholm. "I took some graduate classes there one summer. If you have any spare time when this is over, I'd love to show you around Salem."

Tatyana felt her cheeks blush. "I'd like that."

Dammit, Tatyana chastised herself. *Stop acting like a lovestruck schoolgirl.*

Once on the third floor, Denholm led her into the old master bedroom now used as a library. Shelves lined all four walls, each filled with books ranging from contemporary to volumes dating back hundreds of years. Four wooden tables dominated the floor, each containing two work areas, one on either side and on opposite ends. Laptops sat at each station surrounded by piles of books and papers. Two college-aged men typed away diligently.

"Gentlemen," began Denholm. "This is Tatyana Reynolds from Dartmouth. This is Todd and Matthew."

Todd stood and reached across the table to shake Tatyana's hand. "It's nice to meet you."

"Likewise."

Matthew waved from his seat across the room. "Howdy."

"In addition to giving tours, the guides are required to write papers for the institute on some aspect of the city's history. Todd's working on a piece about blacks living in colonial Salem. Matthew is writing a social history of the city from 1750 to 1850. Matthew is attending Salem University, so his paper will earn him course credit." Denholm motioned toward his office.

Like the previous room, his office had also been converted from a bedroom, only this one much smaller. In the center sat a large wooden desk piled with books. Shelves crammed with books lined the walls. Tatyana quickly glanced across the titles. As predicted, most pertained to Salem or the history of other countries and cities Salem traded with. The shelf behind Denholm's desk contained several books detailing the witch trials and numerous volumes on witchcraft in general and the trials and burnings in Europe. The only empty wall space stood between the twin windows on the exterior wall. Photographs of various locations in Salem and the surrounding cities associated with the trials filled the wall, some of which Alison had shown her yesterday.

Denholm pointed to the seat in front of his desk, a replica of an 18th-century wing-backed chair decorated in red upholstery. As Tatyana sat, she noticed an 8x10 photograph of Denholm with his wife and two young boys, each no more than two, resting in a brass frame.

"Is that your family?" Tatyana tried to hide her disappointment.

"It was." Denholm slid into his modern desk chair. "My

wife left two tears ago and took the boys and the dog back to Rhode Island. Not that I blame her. I spent way more time here than I did at home."

"I'm sorry to hear that."

"It's history, which is ironic." Denholm clapped his hands together, ending the topic. "Alison called last night and said I needed to speak with you, and that you're on a special assignment for the mayor."

"That's right."

"Alison didn't tell me anything, but I assume it has something to do with the witch trials of 1692."

"Why do you assume that?"

"An educated guess." Denholm smiled. "I'm the city's expert on that period of history. And I did an Internet search on you last night and discovered that you're a spirit cleanser."

"At least you didn't call me a ghost hunter."

"I read the reviews and articles on you. You come highly recommended. What impressed me is that I couldn't find any self-promotion, which tells me you're not in this for fame or money."

Impressive, thought Tatyana. *Intelligent and good looking.* "Do you believe in ghosts?"

"Have I ever seen one? No. Do I believe they exist? Of course. You can't be involved in Salem's history and doubt their presence. What do you need my help with?"

Tatyana gave him a brief rundown of what had happened three nights ago to Debbie and her friends as well as last night's encounter with Eliza. She emphasized Eliza's reaction when John and Debbie set the twigs on fire. Denholm listened intently. When finished with the explanation, she asked, "What I want to know is how many witches were burned in Salem?"

"None."

"You don't believe me?"

"On the contrary, I do. There have been stories of hauntings at Pioneer Village since it was built in 1930. It's just that none of the official records or eyewitness accounts from that time indicate any of those accused of witchcraft were burned. The Puritans thought it too barbaric."

"Yet they had no problem hanging them."

"You have to understand the mindset of the village leaders back then," explained Denholm. "The trials took place before the King of England incorporated Massachusetts as a colony. No government rules had yet been established guaranteeing a person's civil rights. No one was versed in judicial law. The judges who presided over the accused were men of the cloth. The only thing they had upon to base their decisions was the Bible, and the Bible made only one mention of witches. Exodus 22;18. 'Thou shall not suffer a witch to live.' In their eyes, they were merely following the will of God."

What Denholm told Tatyana made sense, although it raised more questions than it answered.

Denholm sat forward and rested his elbows on the desk. "I'm fascinated by one aspect of the story. You said you accidentally called the Salem Police officer who came to help you sheriff by mistake."

"Yes."

"And the mention of that title set Eliza off?"

"It enraged her. She tried to strangle him and would have succeeded if Alison didn't intervene."

Denholm leaned back in his chair. "It could be a reference to Sheriff Corwin."

"Who's he?"

"An extremely unlikeable and unpopular man and one of the darker individuals involved in the trials. At the time, the law stated if you were found guilty of a capital crime, you forfeited your property and possessions. Corwin took advantage of that and confiscated the land and personal possessions of those found guilty. Many people in town despised him, so it doesn't surprise me if any remaining spirits held a grudge against him. But again, no records link him to the burning of anyone for witchcraft."

"Which places me back at square one."

"Sorry."

"What about the name Eliza?" asked Tatyana. "Does she appear in any of the official documents?"

"I've studied them thoroughly and that name doesn't ring a bell."

"Damn." Tatyana thought for a moment. "What about the bodies of those executed. What happened to them after they were tossed into the gulley?"

"Rebecca Nurse's relatives snuck in the night of her hanging and spirited away the body... no pun intended. Rumor has it that a few others might have done the same for the deceased. Unfortunately, there is no record of what happened to the rest."

"Could they have been buried where Pioneer Village is now?"

Denholm thought about that question for a moment. "It's possible. The village is only a few miles from Gallows Hill. However, no one reported finding a mass burial site when they built Pioneer Village."

"Once again, I'm back at square one."

"When you went to talk to the spirits at the village, did you sense more than one?"

"Just Eliza."

"You mentioned her spirit was powerful. Could she have overridden the auras of the others?"

"It's possible," said Tatyana. "But if there were other spirits there, I should have been able to sense them even if they had been cowered into submission by Eliza. Why do you ask?"

"That area would have been the perfect place to dispose of the corpses. It was an isolated, wooded area far from the village. No one farmed the land because it was too rocky to grow anything and the water was too shallow to be used as a part of the port district. Anything could have happened there and no one would know about it."

Tatyana wished she had known this earlier. She could have checked out Pioneer Village during the day to see if other spirits resided in the area. Lesson learned.

"I've already taken too much of your time."

"Nonsense. I love talking about the trials." Denholm stood. "It's my dark side showing through."

"Thank you for your time."

"It was my pleasure. And please let me know what you find out. This whole incident fascinates me. Besides, I'd like to see you again."

"So would I."

Tatyana saw herself out, exiting the institute onto Essex Street. Halfway back to the hotel, she heard a voice call out from behind her.

"Miss Reynolds."

She stopped. Matthew raced up to her.

"I'm sorry to bother you. We met a few minutes ago at the institute."

"Matthew, right?"

"Yes." The young man smiled.

"How can I help you?"

"It's more like how I can help you. I overheard your conversation with Denholm. You're interested in knowing about Eliza Adams, correct?"

"You've heard of her?" Tatyana could barely contain her excitement.

"A little." Matthew reached into his pocket and removed a 3x5 index card that he handed to her. It contained a phone number. "Dr. Ian McLean at Salem University has some private papers from that period belonging to Judge Corwin—"

"Judge Corwin from the Salem Witch House?"

Matthew nodded. "I've seen the papers and they mention Eliza extensively."

"In what context?"

Matthew became nervous. "I'm not at liberty to say. But if you call Dr. McLean and let him know why you're interested, he'll probably let you look at them. They'll answer all your questions."

Tatyana wrapped her arms around Matthew and hugged him. "Thank you."

"You're welcome. And please, don't tell Denholm about this unless Dr. McLean says it's okay."

"I won't."

Matthew spun around and headed back to the institute. Tatyana rushed back to the Hawthorne Inn to call Salem University.

CHAPTER SEVENTEEN

TATYANA ENTERED HER hotel room, expecting to be greeted by an overzealous Nostradamus. The dog was not there. Simon must be taking him for a walk. She placed the index card on the desk beside her computer, removed the cell phone from her pocket, and dialed. It rang three times before someone answered.

"Hello?"

"Hi. Is this Dr. Ian McLean?"

"It depends. If you're a tax collector or a telemarketer, then no."

"Excuse me?" Tatyana asked, confused.

"Sorry. I kid a lot. Yes, I'm Dr. McLean."

Tatyana rolled her eyes. Another Nick. "My name is Tatyana Reynolds. Matthews from the Peabody Essex Institute suggested I call you. I'm a spiritual cleanser hired by the mayor to investigate a haunting down at Pioneer Village. Matthew said you might be able to help me with my research."

"Does this involve Eliza Adams?"

Tatyana became excited. "You know what I'm talking about?"

"I do, and I can help. Where are you now?"

"I'm staying at the Hawthorne Inn."

"Good. You're close." A rustling of papers came across the line. "I have classes all day. Can you meet me in my office tonight at seven?"

"Of course."

"Great. I'm in the Sullivan Building, which is on the corner of the campus. My office is on the second floor across from the stairs. I'll see you then."

"Thank you."

The phone clicked. Tatyana did a little dance. She might finally get to the bottom of this mystery.

A knock came from the hall. "Come in."

Simon opened the door. Nostradamus rushed in. On seeing his mistress, he ran over and jumped up, placing his front legs on her chest. Tatyana leaned forward for a face bath. Nostradamus raced over to his bed, jumped on, and rolled around on the comforter.

"I hope he wasn't any trouble."

"Not at all," answered Simon. "I enjoy his company. He's a bundle of energy."

As if he knew they were talking about him, Nostradamus paused long enough to bark once, then shoved his head between the pillows and rubbed his face against them.

Tatyana removed a twenty from her pocket and handed it to Simon. "Thank you for taking good care of him."

"It's my pleasure. He's one of the friendliest dogs I've taken care of." Simon took the money and headed for the door. "I'm on duty until six tonight, so feel free to call if you need anything."

"Thanks."

As the door closed, another familiar voice called out from behind her. "You're popular with the men here in Salem."

"Will you stop sneaking up on me?" Tatyana made no effort to hide her frustration.

"I'm only trying to keep you on your toes."

Tatyana grinned and wagged her finger at him. "Keep it up and I'll surround the room with salt and crystals."

Nick held up his hands in surrender. "You win."

"And what do you mean by 'men here in Salem'?"

"Simon likes you."

"Because I give him twenty dollars every time he walks

Nostradamus."

"And it's obvious Denholm is interested in you."

"How would you know that?"

Nick became self-conscious. "I... I heard you talking about him."

"No, you didn't. I just left Denholm a few minutes ago." Tatyana's eyes lit up. "You were spying on me."

"It wasn't spying. I listened in in case I picked up something you missed."

"But you noticed Denholm was interested in me."

"As much as you were in him."

It suddenly fell into place for Tatyana. "You're jealous."

"What?"

"You're upset that we're attracted to each other."

"How can I be jealous?" Nick sounded defensive. "Even if I felt that way toward you, I'm a ghost. There's no way we could...." For once, he found himself at a loss for words.

"I understand what you're getting at." Tatyana wanted to change the conversation quickly. "Do you know about my meeting tonight with Dr. McLean?"

"Who's that?"

"A professor at Salem University. He has information about Eliza Adams."

"The spirit we encountered last night?"

"The same. He didn't want to talk over the phone. I'm meeting him tonight at seven. He says he has documents that will answer all our questions. Do you want to join me?"

Nick shook his head. "I'll sit this one out."

"Are you sure?"

"Yeah."

"Okay." Tatyana paused. "Nick, is everything cool between us?"

"Of course. I'll swing by later so you can get me caught up."

Tatyana watched Nick leave, passing through into the corridor rather than perform his disappearing act in front of her. She felt terrible about accusing him of being jealous. That would have to wait until later. Right now, she needed to get lunch then do some more research on the witch trials before she met with Dr. McLean.

CHAPTER EIGHTEEN

NICK EXITED THE hotel and headed along Hawthorne Street toward the harbor. As a spectral entity, he could materialize anywhere, and that's how he usually traveled. However, this time he wanted to walk, an old habit from his days among the living when he took a long stroll to clear his head and work through any problems.

Tonight, Nick had a major one to resolve.

Though she didn't mean to, Tatyana struck a nerve when she accused him of being jealous of Simon and Denholm. He had dismissed the comment with his remark about not being able to consummate anything since he could not take corporeal form. Tatyana had dropped the subject, for which he was thankful. Nick did not want to deal with the reality that Denholm did make him intensely jealous.

Nick struggled to understand where the jealousy came from. At first, he assumed it was because he loved her, but ruled that out in the first few weeks of their... what do you call what they had together? A relationship? A partnership? A friendship?

That was part of the problem. Nick did not know how to define what they had. It was deeper than a normal friendship, although nothing about their closeness could ever be considered normal. They only had their age in common, which did not amount to much when weighed against the differences. He came from a generation raised during the Great Depression that then went off to fight World War II. Tatyana came from a generation that felt the world was coming to an end if the WiFi went down for a few days. Nick died fifty years before she had been born and, as such, was more like a grandfather to her. Their life experiences could not be more different.

Nick veered left onto Derby Street and walked down to the port district, the heart of old maritime Salem. He passed by the Salem Customs House, where Nathaniel Hawthorne once worked as a clerk before writing *The House of Seven Gables*, and the brick home of Elias Haskett Derby, Salem's most famous merchant and the first millionaire in America. Salem's past historical spotlight now became its modern counterpart's tourist appeal. The waterfront district served as a reminder to Nick that he and Tatyana were as far removed as contemporary Salem was from its colonial days.

Yet, like Salem, the gap that separated him and Tatyana contained the link that united them – their paranormal experiences.

Nick crossed the street and proceeded down Derby Wharf, which extended a thousand feet into the harbor. He slowly made his way to the light station at the far end. The sound of the ocean breaking against the foundation soothed him. It always had, from when he was a kid up until his tour in the Navy. He focused on the lapping of the waves and the subtle breeze blowing in from the ocean, allowing the sensations to wash away confusing thoughts. The sounds of the ocean cleared his mind and provided him with the clarity he needed.

As his eyes scanned the harbor, he reminisced about his years in the Pacific, which were the happiest of his life… well, living life. Excluding combat, which was terrifying and bowel-clenching, those had been serene years. Sailing the open seas. Visiting countries and ports of call he had never even heard of, and several he wished he never had. The camaraderie of his shipmates and the bonds of friendship that developed, bound by the ugly reality that any day one of them might die in combat. Compare that to what happened when he returned home to Kathleen and experienced betrayal, heartbreak, murder, and eight decades of being tormented by the dement-ed spirit of his wife. Not a tough choice which period of his past life he preferred.

Nick felt the same sense of contentment being with Tatyana that he did in the service. The two of them clicked. He felt at ease around her. Yes, Tatyana was attractive and, if things had been different… if he were alive… he probably would ask her out. They got along, bantered, and worked well together. Granted, cleansing malevolent spirits was not as dangerous as being attacked by a flight of *kamikazes*, but it made for a good retirement job. He and Tatyana were doing what little they good to make the world a better place, and he found happiness in doing so with a good friend.

Then the realization struck Nick. He wasn't jealous of Si-mon and Denholm because they hit on her. He feared that someone might come along that stole her attention, that detracted from the time they spent together. It would be inevitable. One day Tatyana would meet someone, fall in love, and start a family. Deep down, he wanted her to find the solace in life that had eluded him. Hopefully, it would not happen soon. And if his friendship with Tatyana interfered with her life, he would do what he should have after being released from Eden Hollow – leave this realm for the afterlife. Until then, he would enjoy the time he had with her.

Nick hung around the light station for a few minutes before heading back to shore. Halfway down the pier, a couple approached from the other direction, a young man and woman. They were dressed all in black. He wore a black overcoat and boots laced up to his calves. She wore a black t-shirt emblazoned with the Satanic cross and the words Salem Witch Village surrounding it, a black mini-skirt, black boots, and matching nylons. Two nose rings hung from each nostril and three were embedded in her lower lip. As they passed, she met his gaze and said, "Hello."

"Howdy."

Nick stopped. Did she see him? He turned around. The young woman glanced over her shoulder and waved. Nick waved back.

He continued walking, laughing to himself. She had the same ability Tatyana did to see the spirits that still existed in this realm. Three hundred years ago, that skill would probably have meant her execution on Proctor's Ledge. Now she embraced it.

The only constant in life was change.

CHAPTER NINETEEN

30 October 1692
Salem Village

ELIZA SAT AT her dining table and sobbed. It was finally over.

The judges disbanded the Court of Oyer and Terminer yesterday, although not before four more months of trials and executions. The tolerance for such a travesty faded when the accusers tried to widen their web of deceit. In July, Anne Putnam and Mary Wolcott traveled to the adjacent town of Andover to hunt for witches there. However, not knowing any of the inhabitants, they were unable to accuse potential victims. They suggested the touch test in which town residents would place their hands on the girls to see if they reacted. When everyone who touched the two caused a reaction and was accused of being a witch, the town officials put an end to the charade and sent the girls home.

The death knell came earlier in the month when one of the girls accused the governor's wife of engaging in witchcraft. Not surprisingly, the trials stopped and the court was disbanded. Yet the suffering did not end. More than one hundred and fifty accused remained in jail. Those who could afford to pay the costs of their incarceration were released while the poor remained in prison, building up their tab. In an irony that should have surprised no one, all the afflicted girls were miraculously cured of the release of their supposed tormenters. Only time would tell whether those who had engaged in such murderous antics would be punished. Knowing the perverse nature of man, Eliza doubted justice would prevail. However, it was not something she could dwell on.

Eliza had to cope with her contribution to this nightmare.

Eliza stared at the logs burning furiously within the fireplace, generating a soothing warmth she did not feel. Guilt wracked the young woman and left her chilled. She had witnessed each gathering of evidence, each trial by the Court, and each murder. She had watched in shock and dismay as the band of depraved girls performed their machinations before the dumbfounded of Salem Village, each anguished cry and melodramatic shiver condemning another person to the gallows. Throughout it all, she knew the accused were innocent of the outlandish charges brought against them. None of them were guilty of witchcraft because there was only one witch in Salem Village.

Her.

Eliza corrected herself. Witches did not exist, at least not those described in the legal codes of western and central Europe, although the activities she engaged in would indeed have been viewed as such by the Puritans. For centuries, Christianity cultivated the erroneous belief that men and women were born with the ability to cause harm, or *maleficium*, to humans, cattle, or crops by a mere thought or glance, the notorious "evil eye" of legend. They blamed everything, from bad weather and sexual impotence to curdled butter, on consorting with Satan. Sure, she had known people born with unique abilities, abilities that allowed them to talk with spectral entities or foretell the future, but nothing that fell within the legal definition of witchcraft. None of them could cast spells or cause carnage and rarely used their supernatural skills for ill.

Eliza considered herself a white witch, a benign form of sorcery despite the negative connotation associated what that term. Her abilities were not innate but learned over the years, predominantly from her mother and an older sister who died a decade ago in Scotland. Other sorcerers used their powers to harm others. Eliza preferred to use her skills to provide folk remedies to heal the poor and livestock, determine who were maliciously aligning the innocent, and occasionally cast a love spell designed to imbue the timid with a sense of confidence.

Not that any of it mattered. Eliza did not pray to God but to the Great Spirit. She did not look to the Bible for guidance but to her book of spells. She shunned the norms of society. Despite using her skills to benefit the community, the God-fearing Christians of Europe and the colonies made no distinction, brandishing psychics, followers of voodoo rituals, and anyone out of the norm as worshippers and followers of Satan. It had resulted in the hanging of her mother and older sister in Scotland. Eliza had barely escaped with her life, coming to the New World where she hoped to find greater tolerance and acceptance than in the Isles, a hope dashed shortly after arriving in Massachusetts.

Two things sickened her about the past nine months. First, the willingness of the locals to engage in such bloodshed. The frenzy of the locals to blame their shortcomings on their people, their friends, and their neighbors was surpassed only by the lust of those who knowingly condemned them to death for pure attention. Salem Village had fallen apart the past few years. Arguments among neighbors, a weak Reverend Parris who became a man of the cloth only after all his other business ventures failed miserably, Indian attacks on the colony along the coast, and a crisis of faith had shattered the village's cohesion. Rather than look inward at their own failings, most residents saw fit to go along with the hysteria to blame others. Many villagers spoke out against the mayhem, only to find themselves or their loved ones standing in the witness stand. Terror gripped the village that allowed common sense to give way to a mob mentality.

Eliza's inaction sickened her most. She used to pride herself on being a strong-willed and rational woman, yet even she had been culled into submission by events. The proper course of action would have been to admit her dealing in white witch-craft and try to absolve the others of their fate. She told herself that doing so would do little good, that the acknowledgment of her dabbling in what the Puritans considered the occult would serve as a basis to condemn even more people until they found that magic number of forty. It might have been true. That still did not absolve her. The truth was Eliza saw what had happened to the innocent and had remained terrified of the fate that would await her. She had chosen self-preservation and would have to deal with both the shame and the guilt for the rest of her life.

Eliza had made the decision weeks ago that once the nightmare ended, she would move out of Salem Village, sell her property, and move further inland so she could practice her magic where she would be safe and others would not suffer. She would leave in three days. Hopefully, no one would make the connection between—

A cold chill ran down Eliza's spine when she heard the knock on her front door.

CHAPTER TWENTY

THE DRIVE FROM Hawthorne Inn to Salem University took only a few minutes. The university sat on the wedge of land between Lafayette Street and Loring Avenue, less than a mile from Pioneer Village. Tatyana found a parking space on Lafayette Street only a few hundred yards from the Sullivan Building. Locking her car, she crossed the grassy area in front of the building and entered. The Sullivan Building was one of the oldest on campus, a three-story brick structure dating back to 1896. Tatyana made her way to the second floor and found Dr. MacLean's office right across from the stairwell. She knocked.

"Come in." answered the cheerful voice from the other side.

Tatyana entered. The office was large and contained two desks, one by the door and the other by the window. A distinguished man sat at the second desk. He had snow-white hair, well-groomed but slightly frazzled. He wore jeans and sneakers that clashed with his blue dress shirt and black tie with the words Witch City sewn onto it. Four shelves sat on either side of the window. The books that did not fit on the shelves sat in piles on the floor. The professor's desk was the epitome of disarray, with books and papers covering almost every square inch. A lunch box with a red and black plaid design sat open on his blotter. The professor ate apple slices from it.

"Are you Dr. McLean?"

"I am." He removed a pair of thick glasses from his nose, tossed them on the desk, and then stood to greet Tatyana.

"You must be Miss Reynolds. Come in."

As she approached, Dr. MacLean removed a stack of books from the wooden chair beside his desk and motioned for her to sit. He placed the books on the floor, sat down, and turned to his visitor.

"Matthew says you're interested in the Salem Witch Trials."

"Yes. I'm a spirit cleanser. Several days ago, there was an unusual haunting down at Pioneer Village."

"I heard. Four teenagers arrested for trespassing claimed to have seen a ghost there."

Tatyana was surprised. "You know about that?"

"The rumor mill is quite active on college campuses. And I assume you're here to investigate the incident."

She nodded. "The mayor asked me to determine if there is an entity residing there and, if so, get rid of it. I talked with Denholm Goss at the Peabody Essex Institute. He said the city hanged those convicted of witchcraft at Gallows Hill, and no executions took place at Pioneer Village."

"And Matthew told you to come see me because I might have information to shed light on this mystery."

"Yes." Tatyana paused. "I hope I didn't get Matthew in trouble."

"You didn't." Dr. McLean smiled. "Matthew is one of my best students and is helping me on a special project. And he's right. I can help you clear this up."

Tatyana failed to contain her excitement. "That's wonderful."

Dr. McLean opened the lower right drawer of his desk and removed a small safe that he placed on his desk. Removing a key from his pocket, he unlocked it and lifted the lid. Inside sat a worn, leather-bound book that appeared several hundred years old. The professor removed the book and placed it on his blotter.

"This is the unpublished diary of Judge Corwin."

Tatyana recalled the spirit they encountered at the Witch House. "*The* Judge Corwin from the trials?"

"The same. He wrote this from 1662 to 1718. It includes a segment on the witch trials. Judge Corwin requested in his will that it be locked away and never released to the public. About a year ago, a distant relative of the judge found it amongst his grandfather's possessions and brought it to me for authentication. He let me have it. I've been using it to write a biography of Judge Corwin. Once I've published my book, I'm going to donate the diary to the institute." Dr. McLean paused as if re-evaluating his decision. "There's a portion in here that you'll find quite useful for your research. If I let you read it, you must promise me two things. First, that you'll never discuss what you read with anyone until my book is published."

"You have my word," said Tatyana. "What's the second thing?"

"That you come back when this is over and let me interview you for my book."

"It's a deal." At this moment, she probably would have promised her soul to see the contents.

Dr. McLean picked up the diary and opened it to a section he had bookmarked. He handed it to Tatyana.

"You can sit at Dr. Ames' desk to read it."

Tatyana took the diary and rushed over to the other desk, gently placing it down. It was in remarkably good condition for a book over three hundred years old. The pages were yellowed and frayed around the edges, and the print had faded slightly but was still legible. She began reading the entry dated 30 October 1692.

CHAPTER TWENTY-ONE

October 30, 1692

William Haskell came to me this afternoon with the most disturbing news. Haskell is the closest neighbor to Eliza Adams, who lives on the outskirts of Salem Village. Haskell is a kind and quiet man with a wife and three children. He is a regular attendee at Reverend Parris' sermons. I know him by reputation only, and that reputation is good, so I believe everything he has told me and which I write down here.

It all began with a good Christian gesture. William had not seen Ms. Adams for several days and, in light of recent events, worried about her, or so he related to me. He visited her home earlier this evening shortly after sundown but, rather than knock and possibly upset her, he peered through her window to see if Ms. Adams were at home, an intrusion fortunate for us. He witnessed Ms. Adams performing what he termed 'a satanic ritual.' Despite his fear of being caught and what fate may befall him, he watched and gathered details to pass to the magistrates.

William fled and, after stopping at home to warn his family to stay inside and lock the doors, immediately came to me to report what he had observed. He voiced his concern that witchcraft still existed in Salem Village and feared what would befall his family if Ms. Adams ever found out he knew her secret. I assured William I would take care of the matter and keep him and his family out of it, for which he showed great appreciation. We both prayed for divine intervention on our behalf and our salvation. I warned William not to mention to anyone that which he had witnessed and his coming to me, and made him swear on the Holy Bible and in His name to keep this secret. William agreed.

I am appalled that Satanism still thrives in our village. I have pondered and prayed over this for hours, wondering what we had down to anger God so much that he sent such chicanery amongst us. Have we let down the Lord Our Father? Or is he merely testing our Puritan faith as he has with poor harvests these past years? In either case, we must adhere to God's will. Though I, for one, am uncertain what He asks of us.

I sent word to Sheriff Corwin to meet me tomorrow morning to discuss how to resolve the matter.

I will read the Bible and pray for divine protection for the good people of Salem and His guidance. I doubt I will sleep to-night. May the Lord hear my prayers.

October 31, 1692

I slept fitfully. God must be testing me for he offered no resolution. I face the same choices I dealt with last night. Confront Ms. Adams about the charges against her and, if true, punish her according to the Good Book, which could incite again the hysteria that has gripped Salem these past nine months. Or ignore the situation and pray that witchcraft does not again rear its ugly head in our village.

Dear Lord, I need your guidance now more than ever.

Sheriff Corwin just left. My cousin and I often do not agree on matters pertaining to the village. Today's meeting was particu-larly contentious.

I related to him what had been told to me in confidence, leav-ing William's name out of the conversation. I expected him to be as shocked as I was by such a blatant display of Satanism after all we had been through. Instead, he expressed outrage.

"We must purge Salem of this evil," he declared, slamming his hand on the table. He stood and paced my dining room in an agitated state.

"Haven't we gone through enough?"

"You are one of the magistrates of this village, and yet you shirk from thine duty to the citizens you are entrusted to protect?"

"That is not fair," I protested. "You know I have done my duty for the citizens of Salem."

"What about your duty to God?"

The vehemence with which my cousin asked the question shocked me. "We cannot risk starting another round of trials and accusations."

"Cousin, your concerns are admirable. But we have proof that this woman is a witch."

"All we have is the word of a frightened man."

"Then let's get proof." My cousin sat down before me. "We'll go by her house later this evening and search it. If we find evidence of her consorting with Satan, then we have all the proof we need to convict her."

I was torn between my sense of duty and my common sense, my questions from the night before still unanswered. "The village can not afford another round of public trials and hangings."

"Who says it has to be public?"

My cousin's willingness to conspire against the law disturbed me. "What are you saying?"

"The trials were conducted because most of those accused refused to admit to their crimes. This time we have evidence. Did you not say your source was a man of God and reliable?"

"I did."

"Then we search the witch's house tonight. If we find evidence of her dalliances with Satan, you as a judge can pronounce sentence, and I, as the sheriff, can carry out the verdict in private. There is no injustice in that."

I admit I lacked the courage to make such a decision on my own. "We should ask Judge Hathorne what he thinks."

My cousin stormed around the room again in a fit of anger. "He is an old man too feeble of mind to entrust this to him. What is required is action. We are the only men capable of doing this.

No one else needs to know."

I still hesitated, unable to make a decision.

My cousin returned to the chair in front of me. "Will we not be committing an injustice against the villagers we are sworn to protect, and will we not be viewed as sinners in the eyes of God, if we do not punish the wicked for their evil deeds? The Bible says, 'Thou shalt not allow a witch to live.'"

"I don't know."

"We will go by the house later this evening when the village is asleep. If we find no evidence of witchcraft, then no harm is done. If we do find proof, we can resolve the matter by morning."

The truth which my cousin spoke overrode my common sense, and I agreed to his proposal. He left, making me vow to tell no one. I still feel unrest about my agreeing. I will spend the afternoon seeking divine guidance from Our Lord. I hope this time He answers my prayers.

The Good Lord never answered my prayers. How I wished he had considering what happened this evening.

My cousin showed up shortly after sunset with five men and a wooden cart to carry away the prisoner. They seemed determined. I have no idea what my cousin told them, but each man was enraged with anger, though I detected the fear in their tired eyes. I began questioning my cousin's impartiality yet still went with him to confront Ms. Adams. I thought I could be a calming influence if events got out of hand.

The village was silent as we made our way to Ms. Adams' house. No one dared venture forth in the dark, the fears of the last nine months still gripping the village. We made as little noise as possible so as not to attract attention and proceeded to the southern edge of the village where Ms. Adams lived. Twas the first time I had seen her residence. The house and grounds were well maintained, and nothing evident to my eyes indicated any suspicion that Ms. Adams delved in witchcraft.

"See that," whispered my cousin. "There is proof of her rela-

tionship with Satan. How else do you explain a young woman with no husband and no means affording property such as this?"

"That is not evidence," I interjected. "We have no idea of her circumstances."

My cousin glared at me. He spoke respectfully, but I could see the contempt and warning in his eyes even in the dark. "You are here as a magistrate to judge the accused. Let me conduct the trial."

"A light burns in the window," said Jebediah.

"I doubt the harlot is reading the Good Book," sneered Ezekiel.

"Silence," ordered my cousin. "We do not want to warn her of our approach."

We stopped outside the residence. My cousin walked up and knocked on the door three times. He waited two seconds, barely long enough for anyone to answer, before standing aside.

"David, Nathaniel. Bust it open...."

CHAPTER TWENTY-TWO

31 October 1692
Salem Village

THE DOOR TO Eliza's house burst open. The metal latch flew at her, forcing the young woman to duck. The door slammed against the wall and bounced back as five fierce men raced through the opening and spread out across the room, encircling her. Her first reaction was to defend herself. Eliza rushed toward the fireplace and grabbed the poker. Before she could brandish it, two of the intruders grabbed her by each arm and dragged her back across the room, forcing her to sit on a wooden chair. A third man, the tallest and ugliest of the bunch, stood in front of her, removed a pistol, and aimed it at her face.

"Keep struggling. Please."

To emphasize his point, the gunman cocked back the hammer.

Eliza braced herself for the rape she felt was imminent. It would not be the first time. Then a sixth figure entered the room clasping a walking stick in his right hand, a man in his late twenties who seemed much older. He had stern features accentuated by cold, merciless eyes. Eliza recognized him as Sheriff George Corwin, the self-described witch hunter. Even the appearance in the doorway of Judge Corwin, one of the village's magistrates, offered her little hope. She would have preferred the sexual assault.

Sheriff Corwin strolled around the room and examined every item within sight, playing out the intrusion for dramatic effect. "You're up rather late, Ms. Adams."

"Is it now a crime to stay up past sundown?"

"A crime? No. But it is suspicious." The sheriff sauntered over to the table and ran his hand along its surface. "Most people who are awake at this hour are studying the Bible. Yet I don't see one. Why aren't you reading it?"

"I know it by heart."

"Do you? Are you familiar with Exodus 22:18?"

"'Though shalt not suffer a witch to live.'"

"Of course, you would know that verse." The sheriff chuckled. "What were you doing up at this hour?"

"That is none of your concern," Eliza said defiantly.

The brute holding the pistol stepped forward and leveled the barrel at her head. "Watch thy tongue, witch."

Eliza looked past the weapon into the man's scared eyes. "You act tough, but you're nothing but a flock of frightened hens clucking around the coop. If I were truly a witch, you would all be thrashing around the floor gasping your last breaths."

"How dare you speak to—"

"Nathaniel." The tone of the sheriff's voice rapidly deflated the gunman's temper.

"Where is your Bible?" asked the sheriff.

Eliza refused to answer, knowing that admitting to not possessing one would only damn her further.

"You do own a Bible, don't you?"

Eliza remained silent.

The sheriff turned to his cousin. "Judge Corwin, let it be known for the record that the accused refuses to admit to owning a Bible."

"That is not a crime." The judge's response was half-hearted.

"Maybe not, but it serves to confirm the charges against her."

"What charges?" asked Eliza.

"The charge of consorting with Satan, of course."

"I'm being accused of witchcraft?"

"You used that word, not I."

"Who made such accusations against me?"

Sheriff Corwin wandered over to Eliza. "A person of good moral character who, unlike you, believes in God Almighty."

"I demand to know who my accuser is."

The sheriff stood in front of Eliza. "You are in no position to demand anything."

"It is my right."

The sheriff smiled and turned to his cousin. "Judge Corwin, would you like to reveal the name of her accuser?"

The judge lowered his head, averting their gaze.

"I thought so." Sheriff Corwin focused on Eliza. "I will give you one more chance. Where is your Bible?"

Eliza said nothing.

A malicious grin pierced the sheriff's lips. "Gabriel, Jebediah. Search the house."

Judge Corwin stiffened. "Are you certain that is necessary?"

"Cousin, we agreed that I would handle the investigation and you will pronounce the verdict."

The judge again lowered his head and moved to the corner.

The two men rummaged through the room. Eliza watched them intently. They showed no regard for her possessions, spewing the contents of her cupboard onto the floor and kicking them around with their boots. As Jebediah made his way into the other room to ransack her bedroom, Gabriel went over to the fireplace and foraged through her cooking utensils. The other three men maintained their watch on Eliza while the sheriff moved about, reveling in his power. When Gabriel examined the wall to the right of the fireplace, Eliza averted her gaze.

Sheriff Corwin noticed it. "Gabriel, check the area around the fireplace."

He began tapping his knuckles against the wood. When he

reached the third panel to the left of the hearth, his knocking produced an echo.

"Sheriff Corwin, I found something."

Eliza lowered her head. Her death warrant had been sealed.

Sheriff Corwin raced over. Gabriel rapped again, producing the same hollow sound. The sheriff removed the poker from the stand and plunged the pointed end between the wood, prying loose the panel. He yanked it off the wall and tossed it to the floor, revealing a cubby hole built into the frame. A small wooden box sat inside. The sheriff removed it and lifted the lid. His eyes widened.

"What did you find?" asked the judge.

"The evidence we need to condemn her as a witch."

The sheriff walked over to the table and dumped out the contents. Four half-burnt candles, six crystals, two bottles of ointment, and several plants and flowers spilled out. As the sheriff rummaged through them, Judge Corwin came over to investigate. The judge inhaled deeply.

"Dear God."

"God has nothing to do with this," responded the sheriff. "This is the work of Satan."

"I do not consort with Satan," said Eliza.

"These proof otherwise." Sheriff Corwin swept up the sage in his hands. "What are these for? Potions? Incantations?"

"I use them as natural remedies to cure illness."

Judge Corwin shook his head. "That is what prayer is for."

"Sometimes prayer is not enough."

"Witch!" From behind, Ezekiel slapped Eliza on the back of her head. For a moment, her vision blurred.

"Enough," ordered the sheriff.

Gabriel grew agitated. "Sheriff Corwin, come see this."

The sheriff joined his accomplice by the cubby hole and peered in.

Eliza's heart sank. Years ago, her little sister Alese had

made Eliza a doll out of straw and twigs, saying it represented Eliza so she would always have her older sister with her. Eliza had kept it as a reminder of Alese after the mobs in Scotland hanged Alese and her mother for witchcraft. It was the only thing she had left Alese, that and fond memories. It was a token of their affection. However, it resembled a poppy, the tiny dolls witches supposedly used to inflict suffering on their victims, which was why she kept it hidden. Eliza knew it would lead to her conviction.

"What is it?" asked the judge.

"Proof that Eliza Adams is a witch who consorts with Satan."

Sheriff Corwin removed the doll from its hiding place and brought it over to his cousin. He attempted to give it to the judge, but the latter raised his hands and backed away, refusing to touch it.

"Dear Lord, protect us from the evil dwelling in this residence."

Sheriff Corwin smiled. "So, you agree that this confirms Ms. Adams is a witch?"

The judge closed his eyes and nodded.

The sheriff stepped over to Eliza. "You have been found guilty of witchcraft and consorting with Satan. You have committed crimes against man and sins against God. I sentence you to death. How do you plea?"

"I have committed no crime." Eliza's tone was firm.

"I figured as much." Sheriff Corwin moved away. "Jebediah, Gabriel, Ezekiel. Prepare for the witch's execution. We will be along shortly."

The three men did as commanded.

"Samuel, bind the accused."

The man behind her ran out to retrieve rope from the cart. Nathaniel aimed the pistol at her temple. A minute later, Samuel returned and bound Eliza's wrists tightly behind her back.

"Gag her so we don't have to listen to her foul rantings."

Samuel entered the bedroom and came back with a piece of cloth that he shoved into Eliza's mouth, causing her to choke.

"Be careful," warned the sheriff. "We want her alive for her execution."

Samuel adjusted the rag then secured it in place by wrapping a small piece of rope across her open mouth and tying it behind her head. Nathaniel holstered his pistol, then he and Samuel jerked Eliza to her feet and led her outside. Once in the cart, Samuel bound her legs together by the ankles.

Sheriff Corwin led the way. The only sounds came from the creaking of the cart and the occasional snort from the horse pulling it. All the other bugs and animals of the night had gone silent. Even nature, which Eliza worshipped, had abandoned her.

After several minutes, Eliza realized that the caravan was not heading north toward Gallows Hill where the others had been hanged, but proceeded south, away from the village and to an isolated portion of woodland along the rocky shore. They entered the woods. No one spoke. No one taunted her. The solemnity of the situation caused as much fear as her fate.

Eliza's fear turned into terror as the cart broke through the trees into a small clearing. A small bonfire lit the area. She had expected to see a noose hanging from a tree branch. Instead, a ten-foot pole had been erected in the middle of the clearing with timber and broken branches encircling the base, piled three feet in height. The realization suddenly struck Eliza. They were not going to hang her.

They intended to burn her alive.

Eliza struggled against her restraints, only succeeding in toppling to the floor of the cart. She tried to wiggle to freedom, a futile gesture. She screamed, her cries for mercy muffled by the gag.

The cart stopped in front of the pole. As the five men lifted her out and carefully carried her up the pile of timber, Eliza overheard the two Corwins arguing.

"This is not Germany," said the judge. "The accused should be hanged."

"We need to make an example of her."

"What example? We're the only ones who know about this."

"You may leave if you want," snapped the sheriff. "You've already pronounced her guilty of witchcraft. Leave me to carry out the sentence."

As three of the men held her in place, Nathaniel and Samuel lashed her legs, waist, and torso to the pole. The latter removed her gag and they climbed down. The five moved over beside the bonfire.

"This is barbaric!" she yelled.

"Silence, witch." Sheriff Corwin approached. "I will not listen to the ravings of someone who has brought so much misery to the people of Salem Village."

"It's you who have caused the suffering."

"Liar."

"I speak the truth," spat Eliza.

"You led the coven—"

"Coven? All those people you hanged and imprisoned were innocent of the crimes of which you accused them. There is only one witch in this village, and it is I."

"You heard her." Sheriff Corwin turned to face his cousin and his men. "She admitted to practicing witchcraft."

"You want a confession? Fine. I have dealt with white witchcraft. I have used my powers to help the sick and ward off evil."

"You are the evil!" Sheriff Corwin screamed the accusation, his entire body trembling with rage.

"The only evil in this town are those children who sent nineteen people to their deaths while they sought attention and the feeble-minded like yourselves who gave it to them. You have the blood of innocents on your hand, not I."

"Do not listen to her," the sheriff told his men. "Satan speaks through her to protect his followers."

"Kill me if you want, but please hang me."

"Shut thy foul mouth, witch. You will receive the punishment you deserve." Sheriff Corwin faced those by the bonfire. "Carry out the sentence."

As one, the men removed torches from the bonfire and surrounded the base of the poll, repeatedly touching the timber and branches until they ignited. Small fires erupted around the pyre, slowly merging into one. The five men retreated as the flames roared into their full fury, lapping at Eliza's feet. Her dress burst into flames, searing her skin beneath.

Eliza shrieked as her skin melted away.

Judge Corwin raced over to the sheriff. "For God's sake, end this now."

"I am doing God's work," said the sheriff. "Feel free to put onto the flames and hang her."

The judge withdrew, bowing and praying Eliza's suffering would end quickly.

God did not answer the judge's prayer.

The flames climbed higher, setting Eliza's chest on fire. Her skin seared away first, followed by the tissue beneath. She shrieked in excruciating pain until the nerves burned away, sparing her physical agony. However, her blood and bodily fluids started to boil.

Judge Corwin raced over to the pyre, stopping when the heat became unbearable, and dropped to his knees.

"Please forgive us our sins against you."

"Only your God can forgive your sins, so pray to him, though it will do you little good." Eliza's voice was strained and raspy, her throat and vocal cords shriveled from the heat. "I curse this place and will haunt it until justice is done."

"Shut up, witch." Nathaniel withdrew his pistol and fired a single round.

The bullet struck Eliza in the temple above her left eye, blowing off part of the skull. Blood and pieces of brain fell into the flames, sizzling. Yet Eliza remained alive.

Her face blistered, creating bubbles that burst, disfiguring the poor woman. Her body provided fuel, causing the flames to increase in intensity. Eliza gasped one final time, breathing in the heated air that seared away her lungs. Eliza went limp, finally spared from her suffering.

CHAPTER TWENTY-THREE

October 31, 1692

We stayed for an hour until the body had been reduced to ashes and the flames died down. Darkness descended over the clearing, broken only by the light from our bonfire. No one spoke the entire time.

My cousin was the first to break the silence.

"Good job. Disperse the ashes and cover them with water. And remember, no one speaks of this incident ever again." My cousin turned to me, his gaze locking on mine. "No one."

As if I needed to be reminded to keep my silence. I left before the others, ashamed of what I had done and wanting to be alone. On the lonely journey back home, I prayed fervently for my salvation and, I am not ashamed to admit, for the soul of Ms. Adams. Even though she was a witch, she deserved better than the abomination my cousin... we put her through this evening.

I sit at my desk writing this, in shock over what had transpired. Ms. Adams' words still ring in my ears: "All those people you hanged and imprisoned were innocent of the crimes of which you accused them. There is only one witch in this village, and it is I."

What if she spoke the truth? What if those executed and still imprisoned are innocent?

My God, what have we done?

I have repeatedly prayed to God Almighty to forgive me for my sins but am afraid that tonight I forfeited any right to Salvation.

CHAPTER TWENTY-FOUR

TATYANA CLOSED THE diary, her mind still reeling from what she had read. She glanced up. Dr. McLean sat in his chair, staring at her.

"Fascinating, isn't it?"

Fascinating was not the word she would have used. "This is for real?"

"Yes. I've taken great pains to verify its authenticity."

"It's... it's unbelievable."

"Yes, but it's true." The professor gestured toward the diary.

Tatyana handed it back to him. "But I thought there were no witches in Salem?"

"Technically, there weren't." Dr. McLean placed the diary back in the safe, locked it, and returned it to the drawer as he spoke. "At least according to the Puritan definition of witchcraft. It's possible Eliza Adams was a sorceress dabbling in white magic. It was a common practice in Europe at that time. The tradition is carried on this day by Wiccans and those who believe in the powers of crystals. As a psychic, you fall under the category. There are shops scattered throughout downtown Salem that deal in this type of witchcraft." He emphasized the last word by making double quotes with his hands.

"I don't know what to say."

"It's difficult to read. I spent a month wondering if I should even publish my book given that passage."

"But you're still going to do it?" asked Tatyana.

"I'm a historian. The world has a right to know what happened no matter how disturbing the truth may be."

He was right about that, thought Tatyana. If her experiences with the Netherworld had taught her one thing, it was how dark and depraved people could be.

"I hoped reading that passage helped with your research," said Dr. McLean.

"Immensely. Thank you."

"And don't forget our deal."

Tatyana looked at him quizzically. "What deal?"

"That when this is over, you'll come back and let me interview you."

"I promise. But you may get more than you bargained for."

"I hope so." Dr. McLean smiled. "Is there anything else I can help you with?"

"No. The diary answered all my questions."

The professor stood and shook her hand. "It was a pleasure meeting you. I look forward to your next visit."

Tatyana excused herself and made her way back to the car. Her mind raced, still trying to grasp everything she had read. She had told Dr. McLean he had answered all her questions, but that was not accurate. One question remained unanswered.

How would she cleanse Pioneer Village of the spirit of Eliza Adams?

CHAPTER TWENTY-FIVE

TATYANA ENTERED THE hotel and paused. The Tavern on the Green stood across from her. She decided she needed a drink or two. Or three.

Crossing the lobby, she entered. The lounge was four-star and not like the seamy places she and her friends had frequented in her college days. Tatyana found a table in the corner farthest from the entrance and sat in the winged-back chair, her back to the wall. The waiter arrived at the table seconds after she did.

"Can I get you something to drink, ma'am?"

"Yes, please. I'd like a glass of Merlot."

"Would you like to see our selections?"

Tatyana shook her head. "Give me the best brand you have."

"Certainly." The waiter placed a small napkin on the table. "I'll be right back with your drink."

Tatyana rested her elbows on the table, leaned forward, and cradled her forehead in her palms.

"I take it things didn't go well with Dr. McLean."

She raised her head. Nick sat in the chair across from her.

"That would be an understatement." Tatyana placed her cellphone on the table, removed earbuds from her pocket, and connected them to the phone, putting one bud in her ear.

Nick felt insulted. "You're going to use your cellphone with me right here?"

"Of course not." She dragged the cellphone so it sat in front of her. "I'm not going to sit here talking to myself. Unless, of course, you want to appear before everyone in the lounge."

"It would be good for business," Nick joked. "Good idea, by the way."

"Thanks."

The waiter came back and placed the glass of Merlot in front of Tatyana. After he left, she related to Nick every detail she had read in Judge Corwin's diary. He listened intently, becoming more dumbstruck as the narrative progressed. She finished the story and the first glass of wine and then signaled the waiter for a second.

"Let me get this straight," said Nick. "Sheriff Corwin burned Eliza Adams alive?"

"In the woods where the city built Pioneer Village."

"That explains her reaction when you accidentally called the Salem Police officer sheriff."

Tatyana nodded.

"And Judge Corwin did nothing to stop it?"

"He tried, but the sheriff bullied him."

"That explains our encounter with the judge's spirit at the Witch House."

"That's what I thought."

The waiter came over with the second glass of Merlot and took away the old one. Nick waited until he had left.

"And Eliza placed a curse on that area?"

"Her exact words were 'I curse this place and will haunt it until justice is done.'"

"I wonder what she means by justice?" Nick paused. "Do you think she's aware that the judge's spirit still exists in this realm and that she wants revenge?"

"It's possible. We know she's capable of violence." Tatyana reached up and touched the four scratches on her cheek. "However, she didn't say revenge, but justice,"

"Given the circumstances under which she died, it could mean the same thing."

"True."

An awkward silence passed between them.

"What do you intend to do?" asked Nick.

"Cleanse her from that location."

"That sounds dangerous. We both saw what Eliza is capable of."

"I have no choice."

"She's been dormant for over three hundred years."

"I can't take the chance. You saw how she reacted when Debbie made fun of a burning witch. Debbie would probably be dead if we hadn't been there to stop Eliza the second time. Besides, now that she's angered, she may remain violent. And what if she wanders from the village and comes to Salem? We must get rid of her."

"How do you intend to do that? Eliza is going to be difficult to control."

"I haven't figured that out yet." Tatyana took a long sip of wine. "Crystals and salt will not be enough."

"You know I'm with you no matter what you decide."

Nick reached out and placed his hand on Tatyana's. She felt a tingly sensation on her skin.

"I appreciate that. Right now, I'm going up to my room and research this some more."

"Call me if you need me."

"I will. Thanks."

Rather than disappear before her, Nick stood and walked across the lounge, turning into a mist that dissipated by the exit.

As Tatyana finished her wine, she picked up her cellphone and called Alison, getting her voicemail. Tatyana left a message to call her in the morning to tell Alison what she had discovered and plot a course of action. When she put the phone down, it pinged, indicating she had received a text. It was from Denholm.

How about breakfast? I'd like to discuss your case.

CHAPTER TWENTY-SIX

ATYANA LOVED THE idea of having breakfast with
Denholm. They agreed to meet at nine at the Fountain
Place Restaurant on the corner of Essex and Washington
Streets. She arrived ten minutes early. As she approached the
entrance, Tatyana wondered if she had overdressed for the
occasion. She wore a red dress that ended above the knees and
black heels. Although she had told herself in the hotel room her
attire was for her noon meeting with Alison, truth be told, she
had worn this for Denholm.

He had already arrived and grabbed a booth near the door.
Upon seeing Tatyana, he waved her over. She noticed he had
foregone his jeans and sneakers for slacks and dress shoes.
Apparently, he wanted to impress her as well. She no longer
felt self-conscious.

"Thank you for agreeing to see me on such short notice,"
said Denholm as Tatyana slid into the booth opposite him.

"It's my pleasure. I'm glad you called."

The two engaged in idle chatter until the waitress came
over and took their order. When she left, Tatyana focused her
attention on Denholm.

"What did you want to discuss about the case?"

"Nothing. The real reason I texted was that I wanted to see
you again. I hope you don't mind."

"Not at all." Tatyana blushed. "That's sweet."

"Are you going to be in Salem much longer?"

"A few days, maybe longer."

"That's great." Denholm's eyes lit up. "Maybe I can take

you to dinner tonight."

"Not tonight." Tatyana frowned. "We're performing the cleansing ceremony this evening."

"Really?" Curiosity flashed in his gorgeous eyes. "Then I assume your research has gone well."

"I can't go into the details of how I know this, but there was a twentieth person executed for witchcraft at the location where Pioneer Village now stands."

"So, the rumors are true," Denholm said more to himself.

"What rumors?"

"Family rumors. My relatives have lived in Essex County since its founding. Isiah Goss helped establish Salem Town. Benjamin Goss was one of the city's wealthiest maritime merchants. I grew up listening to stories about the family heritage. It's the reason I became a historian."

"And they told stories about executing a witch at Pioneer Village?"

"My great-grandfather did. Mind you, he was almost one hundred when he told me that. He also told me that General Doolittle flew a B-29 off the *Hornet* to drop the A-bomb on Tokyo, so I took everything he said with many grains of salt." Denholm chuckled. "The family also told legends about how one of my relatives single-handedly defeated a British regiment during the American Revolution and another about a relative sailing with Blackbeard, none of which are true. But it makes for good stories."

"I understand. I once investigated a paranormal haunting in which the couple swore demons occupied their house. It turned out to be a family of squirrels living in the attic."

They both laughed, drawing the attention of nearby patrons.

"So, how are you planning on dealing with this ghost?"

"I haven't figured that out yet." The thought of doing so drained much of the joy out of Tatyana.

"Any chance of me attending?"

"I wouldn't advise it. The spirit we're dealing with is particularly malevolent."

"Is that how you got the scratches on your cheek?"

Tatyana turned her head. "Is it that noticeable?"

"Unfortunately. But it doesn't detract from how pretty you are."

Tatyana felt herself blush again. "Thank you."

"Who are we?"

There was no way Tatyana would mention Nick, afraid that would drive Denholm away. "Me and Alison."

"The mayor's assistant. She arranged our meeting yesterday." Denholm grinned. "I'll have to thank her for that."

The waiter arrived with their meals. The couple talked about their jobs and personal lives, sharing stories of their past. Always a gentleman, Denholm paid for her breakfast.

"I have to get back to the office. I have a meeting with the board at ten."

"I hate to see you go."

"I do, too." Denholm stood. "How about dinner tomorrow night? I know this great seafood restaurant down on Pickering Wharf."

"It's a date. And thank you again."

"My pleasure." Denholm squeezed her hand and left.

Tatyana watched him as he left. She had a date with Denholm for tomorrow night.

Assuming she lived that long.

CHAPTER TWENTY-SEVEN

THE MEETING WITH Alison took place in the lobby of the Hawthorne Inn at the same location where they first had met. Tatyana had not changed after her breakfast with Denholm. Alison arrived wearing casual clothes since she was still on paid leave after their encounter with Eliza two nights ago. The bruise on her cheek had grown dark purple and could be seen across the lobby. Upon seeing Tatyana, Alison waved and made her way over. When she drew closer, Tatyana stood and hugged her.

"What was that for?" Alison asked.

"Comradery. We've both been through combat. At least with a ghost."

"You got off better than I did," said Alison, referring to the scratches on Tatyana's face.

"Thankfully, they'll both heal."

"I've been telling people I slipped getting into the shower and hit my face against the wall."

"What about the cop she attacked?"

"John's fine, thank God. He has bruising to the neck and strained muscles but no permanent injuries. The chief gave him the week off to recover."

"What about his report?"

Alison grinned. "He made up a story about someone having hung a noose from a tree and he accidentally ran into it, almost hanging himself. The sheriff bought it. Of course, now he's worked up about systemic racism in Essex County."

"As long as he's not bothering us."

"What did you find out from Dr. McLean?"

Tatyana spent the next forty minutes discussing Judge Corwin's diary and what she had read, answering the occasional question. Alison's face slowly morphed from fascination to awe as she listened to the story unfold. When Tatyana finished, Alison leaned into her wingback chair, silent. Tatyana gave her a few moments to take it all in.

Alison sat forward again. "So, according to this diary, Eliza... the ghost we encountered the other night... was an actual witch who was arrested, convicted, and burned at the stake at Pioneer Village. And this secret has been kept for over three hundred years."

"Yes."

"Is Dr. McLean certain that the diary is authentic?"

"According to him, it is. Everything up to that incident, as well as everything following it, matches historical records. If it's a forgery, it's an elaborate one."

"It does explain why Eliza is so angry and why she reacted the way she did to the witch-burning jokes."

Tatyana nodded. "That's what I'm thinking."

"How do we get rid of her?"

"The usual way. Except this time, I'll do it during the day when Eliza should be at her weakest." Memories of her confrontation with Kathleen still haunted her.

"Sounds good to me," said Alison. "When do we do it?"

"We? I would have thought the other night would have scared you off."

"Normally, it would have. The mayor wants me there to verify you were able to get rid of the ghost. Besides, I'm not going to let you do this alone, not after last time."

"Thanks." Tatyana paused. "I want to conduct the cleansing this afternoon."

"So soon?"

"I want to expel her before she gets more powerful. I have everything I need. There's no need to delay."

"I can't argue that. What time?"

"Four o'clock."

"I'll pick you up here at three-thirty." Alison departed.

Tatyana waited until she left before heading up to her suite. Nick waited for her, sitting on the bed chatting with Nostradamus. The latter jumped down and raced over to his mistress, his tail wagging.

"We're doing it today, then?" asked Nick.

"You were eavesdropping again."

"Just so that I'm up to speed on everything."

Tatyana shook her head good-naturedly. "I'm going to start showering with a bikini on."

"You'd still look sexy." Nick suddenly grew nervous. "Not that I'd know."

"I'm sure you wouldn't." She changed the subject. "Are you ready?"

"I'll be there for you no matter what."

"I appreciate that. Hopefully, this will go well."

"Do you believe that?"

"Yes," Tatyana lied.

"I don't believe you. Anyways, I'll leave you alone. See you at Pioneer Village at four."

Nick stood. He morphed into a mist that disappeared through the window. Nostradamus ran over and barked where Nick had been a second ago.

Usually, Tatyana hated when he did that, but today she let it pass. She had more important things to worry about.

CHAPTER TWENTY-EIGHT

TATYANA HAD BEEN able to take an hour nap, which re-energized her physically and mentally. She woke up a little after two and triple-checked her knapsack to make sure she had all the necessary materials she needed to perform this afternoon's cleansing. As she did, Nostradamus sat beside her, whimpering.

"Do you need to go for a walk?"

The dog stood up and barked.

Putting on his harness and attaching the leash, Tatyana led Nostradamus to Salem Commons, where he peed on the first tree he came upon. They then took a walk around the grounds, Tatyana petting Nostradamus and telling him how much she loved him.

It dawned on her how much the dog genuinely meant to her. She had initially adopted him to help detect any spiritual presences, especially any that visited her apartment. In that short time, Nostradamus had become increasingly important to her. He had become more than a guard dog. He had become a companion and a significant part of her life. She used to chuckle at people on the Internet who referred to their pets as fur babies. Now she understood the sentiment. Tatyana adored him, which was why she would leave him at the hotel this afternoon. Though she refused to admit it to Nick and Alison, she was scared about this cleansing.

Eliza had proven to be the most malevolent spirit she had yet encountered. Her rage was uncontrollable and manifested itself in the ability to inflict injuries on the living. The Salem

Police officer Eliza attacked could easily have been killed. Tatyana feared her safety as well as Alison's. There was a possibility neither of them would survive tonight and, considering she would be the one performing the ritual, the odds were Tatyana would be the one who would die.

Tatyana glanced down at Nostradamus. He paused to do his business on the grass. She bent over to pick it up with a small plastic bag. As she did, Nostradamus licked her cheek.

What would become of him if anything happened to her? Nostradamus loved and relied on her. Until now, she had never considered the possibility he might be left orphaned. She would have to take care of that.

Tatyana led him back to the hotel. Once in the room, Nostradamus jumped on his bed and groomed himself. Tatyana went over to the desk, removed a piece of hotel stationery and envelope from the drawer, and started writing.

To whom it may concern.

If you are reading this, it's because something happened to me this afternoon. The circumstances are not important. What matters is the welfare of my dog, Nostradamus. Please don't send him to a kennel where he may be put down. Please call my friend Julie; I left her number at the front desk. Arrange with Julie to have Nostradamus adopted by her grandmother in Vermont where I know he'll have a lovely home and be properly taken care of. Thank you.

Tatyana

She went over to the bed, sat beside Nostradamus, cuddled and played with him for a few minutes, and told him how much she cared for him. He more than willingly returned the affection.

When the clock read 3:20, Tatyana kissed Nostradamus on the top of his head, grabbed her knapsack and jacket, and went downstairs to meet Alison.

CHAPTER TWENTY-NINE

TATYANA AND ALISON arrived at Pioneer Village a little before four. It appeared much less intimidating in sunlight. However, the two women knew what awaited them inside. Tatyana removed her knapsack from the rear seat. They paused by the front fender, staring at the fence.

Tatyana broke the silence. "Are you ready?"

"I guess. Let's get this over with."

Alison unlocked the gate to Pioneer Village and closed it behind them. They silently made their way to the Governor's Mansion. Tatyana felt Eliza's spectral image enveloping her, filled with rage over their defiance never to return. A cold chill raced down her spine.

Nick stood out front, waiting for them.

"I'm glad you're here." Tatyana placed her knapsack on the ground.

"I wouldn't miss it."

"Are you talking to your ghost friend?" asked Alison.

Tatyana nodded and faced Nick. "Can you materialize so Alison can also see you?"

"Are you sure?"

"Yes."

A moment later, Alison gasped. She quickly recovered and extended her hand. "It's good to meet you in person... or in spirit finally."

"I would shake it but I can't."

"Oh, sorry." Alison quickly withdrew her hand. "This is all so weird to me."

145

"You get used to it," joked Tatyana.

Tatyana opened the knapsack and removed several containers of salt and a box of Selenite crystals. She poured salt over the protective circle she had used two days ago. The original four Selenite crystals remained. She added four more between them and stood back.

"Your job is to protect Alison from the malevolent spirit residing at this location. I know you'll do as I ask."

Picking up the knapsack, Tatyana approached the Governor's Mansion. Alison followed. As Tatyana drew near, Eliza's displeasure made itself known. The negative vibe pounded inside Tatyana's head, generating a constant throbbing.

"I don't feel good," said Alison.

"Go back with Nick. This will only take a few minutes."

As Alison walked away, Tatyana removed a container of salt. Starting with the front left corner, she poured it along the foundation, continuing the process until she had encircled the building.

"Your job is to protect this property from all spirits, benign and malevolent. Once the spirit residing in this building has departed the structure, you are not to allow it or any other entity back inside. I know you'll do as I ask."

Tatyana removed the box of Selenite crystals, placing one at each corner of the Governor's Mansion and on either side of the door, pushing them into the dirt and covering them.

"Your job is to be the watchtower for this property. Assist the salt circle in protecting this building from all spirits, benign and malevolent. Once the house is cleared, you are not to allow any spirits back onto the property. I know you'll do as I ask."

Tatyana walked around the property's perimeter, burying Selenite crystals every five feet along the fence, and then recited the protection stance again. She returned to the protective circle and placed the knapsack inside it. Her headache stopped once away from the structure.

"Alison, get inside the circle where you'll be safe."

"Don't you want me to stay with you?"

"Out here, you're vulnerable, which makes my job more difficult."

Alison stepped inside the circle.

Tatyana approached the Governor's Mansion, stopping several feet in front of the door. The negative vibe pounded in her head again.

"Eliza Adams, you are not welcome here. I demand you leave this building and this area and never return."

The rage from inside the building intensified, but Eliza did not show herself.

"Eliza Adams, do you hear me? You are not welcome here. I demand you leave this building and this area and never return."

Still nothing.

"Why is she ignoring you?" Alison called from the circle.

"Maybe she's afraid to leave the mansion for fear of being banished."

Nick shook his head. "She's defiant. She refuses to confront you in daylight when you're most powerful."

Tatyana stepped up to the door and pounded three times.

"Eliza Adams, I banish you from this building and this compound and forbid you from ever returning."

The negative vibe from the mansion faded.

"It's not working," said Nick. "She's closed herself off to you."

"Damn."

Alison joined them. "What's wrong?"

"Eliza won't confront me during the day."

"That means we have to do this again tonight?"

"I'm afraid so," Nick answered.

Alison swore under her breath.

"Two can play this game," Tatyana had a cold determination in her tone, "I'll challenge her tonight. But I'm going to up the ante."

"What do you mean?" asked Nick.

Tatyana turned to face him. "You stay here and keep an eye on the mansion. Alison and I have an errand to run."

CHAPTER THIRTY

TATYANA AND ALISON took a little over two hours to obtain what they needed and prepare it for the cleansing ritual. Nick kept guard, making sure Eliza did not make a sudden appearance. Half an hour of daylight remained. Tatyana recited the summoning incantation one more time but without success. Rather than make another futile attempt, the three waited by the benches in front of the Governor's Mansion as the sun descended toward the horizon. Tatyana removed four battery-powered lanterns from her knapsack and lit them, placing two by the protective circle. She and Alison carried the last two.

Alison nervously tapped her right foot on the ground. Her left hand trembled. Every few seconds, she would either wipe her sweaty palms along her jeans or glance over at the mansion.

"You can still go home," said Tatyana. "No one will think any less of you if you do."

"I will."

Tatyana placed a reassuring hand on Alison's shoulder. "I know the mayor wants you to be here to witness the ritual. You can turn on your cell phone and leave it propped up somewhere to record everything."

"He'll fire me if I'm not here to witness everything. But that's not why I'm staying." Alison made eye contact with Tatyana. "I've seen what Eliza is capable of. I'm not going to leave you to fight her alone."

Nick waved from a few feet away. "Hello. Right here."

Tatyana ignored him. "Thank you, but you're not trained for this. There's not much you can do."

"Not much is still better than nothing." Alison forced a grin.

Tatyana patted her hand.

"We might want to start the ritual now." Nick pointed toward the shore.

The tip of a full moon had crested the eastern horizon, its image reflecting off the ocean. It appeared unusually large and glowed with a reddish hue, making the moonrise magnificent.

And ominous.

"Isn't that a sugary shit frosting on top of a fucked-up cupcake," said Alison with a slight southern twang.

Tatyana and Nick stared at her. Alison smiled.

"Sorry. I was born and raised in Florida. I lost my accent and my grandmother's old sayings when I came up north. It still leaks out when I get nervous."

Nick chuckled. "I want to hear her recite the incantations."

Tatyana focused her attention on Alison. "Get inside the protective circle and stay there unless I tell you otherwise."

Alison complied. Tatyana removed four abalone shells and four sage bundles from her knapsack, placing one shell on each compass heading. She dropped sage in each shell and lit them, adding to the protective spell.

She turned to Nick. "Are you ready?"

"Let's do this."

Tatyana positioned herself between the Governor's Mansion and the protective circle then raised her arms over her head.

CHAPTER THIRTY-ONE

"**E**LIZA ADAMS, YOU are not welcome here. I demand you leave this building and this area and never return."

Tatyana felt barely restrained anger emanate from inside the Governor's Mansion. Eliza refused to appear.

"Eliza Adams, I know you can hear me. You are not welcome here. I demand you leave this building and this area and never return."

The anger intensified.

"Eliza Adams, I ask that you come out and talk to me. I mean you no harm."

Contempt mixed with fury poured from the mansion.

"Eliza Adams, this is your last chance to meet with me on mutually acceptable terms."

Nick moved alongside her. "I guess it's time for Plan B."

Tatyana sighed. "This is going to be fun."

"I got your back."

The errand she and Alison had run this afternoon had been to Home Depot. They had purchased a ten-foot-long 4x4, ten bundles of firewood, four bottles of lighter fluid, and a lighter. They had planted the 4x4 in the ground in front of the mansion and surrounded it with the firewood, dousing the latter in lighter fluid. In essence, they had created their version of the pyre on which Sheriff Corwin had executed Eliza.

Tatyana removed the lighter from her pocket, lit it, and placed the flame against the firewood. The fluid caught fire instantly, spreading around the base until it created a bonfire that lit the area. She backed away as embers lofted into the night.

The fire had the desired effect.

An ungodly howl echoed from inside the mansion. A glowing light appeared in the upper left window, changing from a luminescent white to reddish-orange. Rather than descend the stairs and exit from the front door as she usually did, Eliza's spirit burst through the wall. Her face had already morphed into its demonic form. The twisted and demented visage. The scraggy hair. The charred and blistered skin. The distorted mouth with blackened teeth. Eliza's eyes glared red. She floated to the ground, stopping a few feet in from of Tatyana.

Tatyana and Nick stood their ground.

"How foolish are you? You defied me by coming back here. And now you taunt me again."

"I'm not taunting you," Tatyana responded. "You refused to talk to me, so I used this to get your attention."

"You have my attention. And now you'll suffer for it."

"I know what happened to you here on that night in 1692."

The rage within Eliza lessened slightly. "What do you know?"

"That you were accused and tried for being a witch in a sham trial in your own home. That you were bound and gagged and brought here to be burned at the stake for your alleged crime. That you were taunted and tormented by your captors as they burned you alive. And that one of your jailors shot you, not to put you out of your misery but to silence your protests against them."

Eliza's glow diminished in intensity and softened to a yellowish hue. "How do you know all this?"

"Judge Corwin kept—"

Eliza roared. "Do not speak the name Corwin in front of me!"

"The judge kept a diary and documented that night in detail."

"Then why doesn't anyone know the truth about what

happened?"

"Judge… he was so appalled by his participation in your execution he never revealed his diary to anyone. It was only recently discovered."

Eliza sneered. "Typical of that spineless abomination of a man."

"The judge's spirit still haunts his house," added Nick.

"Forgive me if I do not pity his tormented soul." Eliza's tome oozed with sarcasm. She scrutinized Nick. "You are one of us. Why do you consort with the living?"

"Tatyana is here to help you and I help her. Like you, I was once condemned to a place I didn't like because of the violence done to me. Through her, I found solace."

"I don't want solace," answered Eliza. "I want justice."

"What do you mean by justice?" asked Tatyana. "Are you seeking revenge on those who murdered you?"

Eliza turned from Nick and laughed derisively. "Those who wronged me are long since dead and have met their fate. What good would revenge do me now?"

"Then what do you want?" asked Tatyana.

"To have my story told. Every other person accused and executed for witchcraft is well known to history. They've been exonerated of their alleged crimes. I suffered the same injustice as they did, yet I am unknown to history and am condemned here for all eternity, doomed to watch people make fun of my demise."

"Were you a witch?" asked Tatyana.

"Not in the sense those frightened Puritans viewed witchcraft. I was born with certain psychic abilities, much like you. Yes, I dabbled in spells, but for the good of the community. I healed the sick. I never killed livestock, destroyed crops, or brought about Indian attacks. And I never once afflicted those damnable children, may their souls be tormented. Yet I am condemned to roam this miserable plot of land for eternity."

"I can help with that," Alison called from the protective

circle.

Eliza studied her for a moment, "Ye, come here."

Alison hesitated.

"I shalt not harm you. You have my word."

Alison left the safety of the protective circle and approached the others. Her body trembled from fear, but she presented a solid façade to the spirit.

"How can you help me?"

"I want to release you from this place."

Eliza sneered. "For your own selfish reasons."

"In part, yes. But you are the twentieth victim of the trials and your story deserves to be told. Your story should be told, and it will be."

Tatyana nodded in agreement.

Eliza's gaze focused on Alison and back to Tatyana. "And you can release me from here?"

"All I need is for you to cooperate."

Eliza turned to Nick. "Can I trust the living?"

"These two, yes."

Eliza's glow softened to a soft white and her visage returned to that of the young woman. "Then I agree."

Tatyana and the others took a step back from the spectral entity.

"Eliza Adams, you were wrongly accused of a crime you did not commit and were executed unjustly. I free your—"

A familiar voice from off to their left distracted them.

"Dear God, the rumors are true."

Denholm Goss stood on the footbridge leading to the Governor's Mansion, an expression of shock on his face.

CHAPTER THIRTY-TWO

"**W**HAT IS HE doing here?" snapped Alison.

"I didn't invite him," Tatyana replied defensively.

"Don't blame her." Denholm left the footbridge and came over to join the others. "She only mentioned in passing that she would be performing the cleansing tonight. I came to see if the rumors were true."

As he approached, Eliza eyed him warily. Her coloring changed back to yellow. Although she had no idea why, Tatyana sensed he was in danger.

"What rumors?" Alison's eyes shifted between Denholm and Tatyana.

"There have been rumors in my family going back generations that a woman was burned at the stake here for the crime of witchcraft. I never believed them until now."

Eliza's aura shifted to bright red. "I know you."

Only Tatyana heard it. She finally put it all together.

Alison was confused. "Why would your family have such rumors?"

Denholm turned to Eliza. "Because one of my relatives, Nathaniel Goss, was here that night."

"Nathaniel Goss?" Eliza's eyes widened in fury. "He was the one who shot me. And you came here to mock me."

"I came to see if the rumors were true."

"They are. And you'll pay for your ancestor's inhumanity."

Eliza morphed into her demonic form and lunged at Denholm. He took several steps back but to no avail. Eliza wrapped her hands around his throat and began to strangle

155

him.

Tatyana ran over. "This isn't the justice you said you wanted."

"On this one, I want *revenge*."

Tatyana grabbed Eliza's hands and attempted to break the latter's grip. With her left hand, Eliza struck out, her hand slapping Tatyana in the face. She flew several feet across the area and landed on a patch of dirt, stunned. Blood flowed over her lips and down her chin. .

"Alison, get back to the protective circle now."

Torn between her desire to help and terror at what was happening, Alison finally obeyed Tatyana and retreated to safety.

Denholm called out for help, his cry an anguished gasp.

Nick moved in and wrapped his arms around Eliza, trying to pull her away. She glanced over her shoulder, her crimson eyes digging deep into his soul.

"You shouldn't even be here," Eliza snarled.

Nick felt his spirit rendered asunder. He devolved into a mist that Eliza blew away, rematerializing on the far end of the compound. As hard as he tried to pull his spirit together, he was unable to do so. Nick could only watch the attack play out from a distance.

Eliza pulled Denholm closer to her. "You wanted to know if the rumors about my death were true? Well, you got your answer. Let me show you the torment I endured at the hands of your ancestor."

Eliza dragged Denholm over to the burning pyre and tossed him on it, placing herself on top of him so he could not escape. The flames formed around her, generating a ghastly image, a spectral fire. Denholm's clothes and hair ignited. He tried to scream but could not, still gasping for breath.

Tatyana climbed to her feet and rushed over to the protective circle.

"We have to help him," shouted Alison.

"It's too late for Denholm. We have to stop Eliza." Tatyana reached into her knapsack and removed a canister of salt. "Stay here."

Tatyana raced back to the pyre. Alison followed.

Opening the container, Tatyana poured a circle around the pyre and, when finished, stood back three feet.

"Eliza Adams, you are now trapped within this circle and cannot move beyond its boundaries."

Eliza spun around and glared at Tatyana. When she released Denholm, he rolled out of the fire onto the dirt. His clothes and hair burned furiously. The flames had charred his body. He reached out a scorched hand toward Tatyana and gasped out a single word.

"'Elp."

Alison slipped off her jacket, tossed it over Denholm, and rolled him outside the circle of salt. The flames caught the sleeve of her blouse. Once Denholm was clear, she tapped out the fire and, ignoring the searing pain in her arm, used the jacket to extinguish the flames that engulfed him.

Eliza noticed none of it, her rage focused entirely on Tatyana. The spirit attempted to lunge but was held in place by the salt.

"What do you mean by this?" Eliza bellowed. "You said you wanted to help me."

"You're beyond help. You allowed the injustice done against you to fester into evil. In the name of all that is good and holy, I banish you from here and command you never to return."

Eliza laughed sardonically. "All that is good and holy? I'm a sorceress. Those powers you invoke have no control over me."

Nick had regained his spectral form and joined Tatyana.

"Normal incantations won't work on her. She abandoned religion for white witchcraft."

Tatyana stepped up to the circle and placed her face mere

inches from Eliza.

"I call on the Great Spirits of the land to fight the perversion of white magic into darkness. Eliza Adams has forsaken what she stands for. Remove her powers and banish this evil through time and space."

"No!"

The trees around the compound groaned and swayed as if bending in the wind, only the night air remained calm. In the light generated by the pyre, Tatyana saw the trees leaning toward Eliza.

Eliza turned to the trees. "You can not do this to me. I'm your friend."

"You lost their friendship when crossed the threshold from good to evil. I banish you from here."

A wind blew from the surrounding trees, focusing on the pyre and fanning the flames. They washed over Eliza, only this time igniting her spectral form. Eliza screamed, reliving the torment that had killed her over three hundred years ago. She focused on Tatyana, her demonic features twisted in hatred and her eyes blazing with rage.

"If I ever find a way to return to this realm, I'm coming for you."

"I won't hold my breath." Tatyana moved away several yards. "By the power of Great Spirits that walk this land, be gone from here and never return. May your afterlife be what you deserve."

The pyre intensified, blotting out Eliza. An anguished howl came from within. A fireball formed and rocketed into the sky, disappearing after a few hundred feet. A burst of wind accompanied its departure, extinguishing the flames and knocking over Tatyana.

A calm descended over the area.

"Is she gone?" asked Alison.

Tatyana closed her eyes and concentrated. "I don't feel her presence."

"She's gone," agreed Nick. "All I detect is a slight residue of Eliza, like a fart in the mess hall."

"Your friend has a way with words," said Alison as she turned her attention back to Denholm.

"Yes, he does." The disapproving look she flashed Nick belied how grateful she was to have him there by her side.

The blaring of sirens and the warning horns of a fire engine broke the silence. Two fire trucks, three Salem Police squad cars, and an ambulance rushed into the parking lot, stopping in front of Pioneer Village.

CHAPTER THIRTY-THREE

TATYANA SPENT HALF the night with the Salem Police, letting Alison do all the explaining. The medics rushed Denholm to Salem Hospital, the main EMT noting it was a miracle he was still alive. They gave Tatyana and Alison a quick exam. Thankfully, Eliza had not broken her nose, but they warned her there would be swelling and bruising in the morning. Alison had suffered first and second-degree burns on her arm but, having caught it in time, she should heal fully with no scars. With the ordeal with the authorities behind her, Tatyana returned to the hotel and spent the night sleeping restfully with Nostradamus cuddled up beside her.

In the morning, she showered and checked herself in the mirror. Her nose had doubled in size, and the area was black and blue stained with splotches of purple. Between that and the scratches on her cheek, she looked like she had gone several rounds in the UFC ring.

She tore up the letter she had written the day before and tossed it in the wastebasket, grateful she did not need it. The encounter last night had been a close one. Many more incidents like these and she might retire early. If she lived that long. When she did give up the business, she would write about her encounters and live off the royalties and movie rights.

Halfway through packing, a knock sounded on her door.

"Come in."

Alison entered. Dark circles appeared under her eyes, and bandages swathed her left arm.

"Thank you for trying to save Denholm last night."

Tatyana did not know what else to say.

"It was the least I could do. I just came from visiting him at the hospital."

"How is he?"

Alison sat on the edge of the bed and sighed. "Not good. He has second- and third-degree burns over eighty percent of his body and his lungs were seared by breathing in flames. He's on life support, but the doctors don't expect him to live more than two days."

Tatyana felt a pang in her chest. "I should go see him."

"Don't bother. The doctors have him in a drug-induced coma." Alison paused. It seemed like she wanted to say something else but could not bring herself to.

"What did the mayor say?"

Alison rolled her eyes. "He chewed me out for an hour this morning. I almost lost my job, though, at this point, I don't care. He's not happy that the police and fire departments had to be called in because now he has to make up excuses for what happened."

"Why doesn't he tell them the truth?"

"That you and I nearly burned down Pioneer Village trying to exorcise a demon from the grounds? The media would eat him alive."

"That's what happened."

Alison nodded in agreement. "That's the only thing that saved me from being canned."

"What now? Is he going to go public with the truth about Eliza?"

"No. He's afraid it would tarnish the city's image. He told the police we were there investigating supposed paranormal activity but found nothing. Denholm built the fire to help with the ritual and accidentally fell in. He swore them all to secrecy. The story he plans to release this afternoon is that kids broke in trying to conjure the ghost Debbie and the others saw. He's closing Pioneer Village for a few months to beef up security and clear the grounds of our activity. He's determined to keep this secret."

"What if one of those who were there last night talks?"

"Not likely, if they want to keep their jobs. Which brings up another topic." Alison hesitated and fidgeted on the bed.

"What is it?"

"Since you signed an NDA when you took on this job, you can't talk about any of this as well, otherwise the mayor will sue you."

Tatyana tried to make light of it. "Well, there goes my idea for a book deal."

"I know. I'm sorry."

"I'm joking about the book deal. I never discuss my work with anyone other than my clients."

"Thank you." Alison met Tatyana's gaze. "Are you mad at me?"

"Of course not."

Alison smiled. "Good."

"It'll all come to light when Dr. McLean publishes Judge Corwin's memoirs."

Alison massaged her temple. "Don't get me going on that. The mayor wants to file an injunction preventing him from publishing the book."

"That'll never happen."

"I know. I'm trying to talk him out of it, telling him a lawsuit will only bring unwanted attention to the matter. Politicians can be frustrating at times. Not that it matters. Eventually, the truth will come out, as it should. Let history decide." Alison stood and walked over to Tatyana. "Thank you for everything."

"I told you I'd cleanse the spirit."

"Not just that. For not lying to me. For allowing me to be a part of this. And for keeping me safe. Meeting you was the only good thing about this whole incident."

Alison moved close to Tatyana and hugged her tight, holding it for several seconds before breaking her hold and kissing Tatyana on the cheek.

"I hope we cross paths again."

With that, Alison left the room.

"Wow," Nick said from behind her. "That was intense. I was hoping for—"

"You even suggest what you're about to and I'll slap you."

Nick waved his hand through the spectral image of his face. "Sorry. Won't work on me."

Tatyana grunted in frustration and went back to packing.

"Are we heading home?" Nick asked.

"Soon. I want to get out of Salem as fast as possible. But I have one thing to do first."

"I'll meet you back at your apartment later."

"Good." Tatyana stopped packing. "Nick, thank you for being here for me. I couldn't do this without your help. You're a good friend."

"My pleasure." Nick would have blushed if he had been able to. "Do I get a kiss on the cheek?"

"Go!"

Nick dissolved into a mist that dissipated through the window. Nostradamus raised his head.

"I'm going to kick his ass someday."

Nostradamus barked his approval.

✕   ✕   ✕

AFTER CHECKING OUT and loading her luggage and Nostradamus in the car, Tatyana drove to Salem University and parked near the Sullivan Building. She exited the car, taking with her Nostradamus and a brown paper bag. Once inside, she made her way to the second floor and knocked on the door to Dr. McLean's office.

"Who is it?"

Tatyana opened the door and entered.

"Tatyana, it's good to see you again."

"I hope you don't mind if I brought my dog along. I didn't want to leave him in the car."

"It's quite alright. I have two dogs at home. How can I help?"

Tatyana sat in the empty chair by his desk and removed a bottle of Merlot and two red Solo cups from the bag. She opened the bottle and poured wine into each cup.

"I promised you I'd tell you about what happened during the cleansing ritual. Only you can't publish what I tell you because I signed an NDA. This is for your ears only."

"I'm happy you thought of me." Dr. McLean took his cup and raised it in a toast. "Here's to revealing a forgotten part of history."

Tatyana tapped her cup against his. "I hope you have a few hours."

A Thank You to My Readers

In addition to working for the CIA, writing has been of the two most fulfilling things I've done with my life. The best part is having fans who read my books, enjoy them, and want more. I'm incredibly fortunate and grateful that I have such a loyal fanbase. You keep reading, and I'll keep writing.

If you enjoyed *The Ghosts of Salem Village*, please post a review on Amazon and/or Goodreads. Reviews are what drive the algorithms that get a writer's books more exposure on Amazon. It doesn't have to be lengthy—just a rating and a sentence or two about why you liked or disliked it. To be successful in this genre, I need your support.

If you enjoyed this book, be sure to pick up the first book in the series, *The Ghosts of Eden Hollow*. I plan to continue the adventures of Tatyana and Nick, but first, I'm concentrating on another project.

Thank you all in advance.

Acknowledgments

The fun part of my job is writing. The difficult part is getting my books published. It's a complicated process involving many people, all of whom deserve to be recognized.

A huge debt of gratitude goes to Rhian Lockard. When I started researching *The Ghosts of Eden Hollow*, I had little understanding of the paranormal. Rhian spent an hour with me on the phone one evening explaining the reality of spiritual hauntings and spectral cleansings and answering all my questions. The background was instrumental in writing these books. She's been extremely supportive. Any errors in how to perform a cleansing, or any intentional diversions from reality for the sake of literary license (such as allowing spectral images to adopt corporeal form or mentally merging with a living person), are all on me.

Before I chose the Salem Witch Trials as the subject of this book, I weighed the decision carefully. I'm a historian by training and did not want to alter the history of this period. I did extensive research on the topic, but the book I found most valuable was Rebecca F. Pittman's *The History and Haunting of Salem: The Witch Trials and Beyond.* Pittman conducted extensive research on the witchcraft hysteria that possessed Salem in 1692, including reading the original court documents and eyewitness accounts of the proceedings. I based the historical portions on this book from *The History and Haunting of Salem.* It is the most detailed, accurate book on the trials I have read; I highly recommend it for anyone wanting to know more about this time.

A major thanks goes out to my beta readers who have been with me from book one: Michael Atkinson, Pammy Troupe, Tom Williamson, Dan Uebel, Norma Seitz, Roseann Powell, Doc Fried, Paul Semke, and Cari Laffrenier Thompson. They point out grammatical/spelling errors, plot flaws, inconsistencies, and offer their opinion on whether they like the story. I would be lost without them.

Warren Design created the cover art for both *The Ghosts of Eden Hollow* and *The Ghosts of Salem Village*. Their work perfectly fits the mood of this book. I'm looking forward to working with them in the future.

Finally, a major debt of thanks goes to my family, human and furry. While working from home allows me to set my hours, the pets are always there as my muses and distractions. Walther and Bella sit with me on my porch while I write during the day (except in the freezing weather when they abandon me for a warm bed) and, at night when I'm in my study editing and managing social media, my cats Archer and Michonne stand in front of my desktop, Michonne because she wants to be petted and Archer to meow because he ran of treats or because he can see the bottom of his food dish. Being a workaholic, I constantly put in more than forty hours a week. My family never complains (I think they're glad to get rid of me). I couldn't do this without their love, patience, and support.

About the Author

Scott M. Baker was born and raised in Everett, Massachusetts and spent twenty-three years in northern Virginia working for the Central Intelligence Agency and traveling through Europe, Asia, and the Middle East. Scott is now retired and lives outside of Concord, New Hampshire, with his wife and fellow writer Alison Beightol, his stepdaughter, two rambunctious Boxers, and two cats who treat him as their human servant. In addition to his paranormal series, he is currently writing the *Nurse Alissa vs. the Zombies* saga, his latest zombie apocalypse series. Previous works include the *Shattered World* series, his five-book young adult post-apocalypse thriller about a group of adventurers attempting to close interdimensional portals into Hell; *The Vampire Hunters* trilogy, about humans fighting the undead in Washington D.C.; *Rotter World, Rotter Nation,* and *Rotter Apocalypse*, his first post-apocalyptic zombie saga; *Yeitso*, his homage to the giant monster movies of the 1950s that he loved watching as a kid; as well as several zombie-themed novellas and anthologies.

Please check out Scott's social media accounts for the latest information on future books, upcoming events, and other fun stuff.

Facebook: facebook.com/groups/397749347486177
Scott M. Baker's Amazon Authors Page:
amazon.com/~/e/B003N4U9BK
Twitter: twitter.com/vampire_hunters
Instagram: instagram.com/scottmbakerwriter
Blog: scottmbakerauthor.blogspot.com